"Why Did You Really Agree To Come Out With Me?"

He leaned in and his lips hovered close to her ear as he added, "If this is you trying to persuade me to sell you the manuscript, it's going to take more than just one date."

Vanessa jerked back, a frown marring her forehead, cheeks coloring as she glared at him. "Two dates, then?"

His deep chuckle aroused her as his warm breath fanned over her cheek. She bit her lip to stop a groan escaping.

"You are something, Vanessa Partridge. But you're definitely not the type to offer yourself up, *Indecent Proposal*-style, am I correct?"

"You…" She had to close her eyes to gather her wits as her heartbeat quickened. "You don't know that."

He eased back to study her. "So what are you offering?"

Her eyebrows went up. "What do you want?"

Dear Reader,

When I was at school, we didn't have a "popular" group—it was more like a "loud and obnoxious" group. :-) Now I'm in Romance Writing World, and rubbing shoulders with writers I read, admire and generally want to be when I grow up. So when I was asked to join *this* particular group—which includes some of my favorite Harlequin Desire authors—I couldn't say no!

So I started Chase and Vanessa's story with my most favorite part of writing—delving deep into their pasts to discover what makes them tick. Vanessa's baggage seemed to fall into place a lot easier than Chase's…. That man just wouldn't give up his secrets easily! But when I finally pieced together his childhood, everything else started to flow. And as always, I did a lot of surfing (read: research) and discovered some fascinating websites on New York, Washington, hedge funds, the Library of Congress… Now I desperately want to see it in real life and not just via Google Earth!

I hope this story comes alive for you, this fourth book in The Highest Bidder continuity. I had such a great time writing it. I'd love to hear from you at www.paularoe.com!

Paula

PAULA ROE

A PRECIOUS INHERITANCE

HARLEQUIN®
entertain, enrich, inspire™

Special thanks and acknowledgment to Paula Roe
for her contribution to The Highest Bidder miniseries.

Recycling programs
for this product may
not exist in your area.

ISBN-13: 978-0-373-73199-2

A PRECIOUS INHERITANCE

www.Harlequin.com

Printed in U.S.A.

Books by Paula Roe

Harlequin Desire

Bed of Lies #2142
A Precious Inheritance #2186

Silhouette Desire

Forgotten Marriage #1824
Boardrooms & a Billionaire Heir #1867
The Magnate's Baby Promise #1962
The Billionaire Baby Bombshell #2020
Promoted to Wife? #2076

Other titles by this author available in ebook format.

PAULA ROE

Despite wanting to be a vet, choreographer, cardsharp, hairdresser and an interior designer (although not simultaneously!), British-born, Aussie-bred Paula ended up as a personal assistant, office manager, software trainer and aerobics instructor for thirteen interesting years.

Paula lives in western New South Wales, Australia, with her family, two opinionated cats and a garden full of dependent native birds. She still retains a deep love of filing systems, stationery and traveling, even though the latter doesn't happen nearly as often as she'd like. She loves to hear from her readers—you can visit her at her website, www.paularoe.com.

This book would never have come about without two groups of people: first, the fabulous Harelquin Desire editorial team (Jessica and Liba for their awesome editing, and Charles, who has the delightful task of answering all my questions and queries and fielding my out-there ideas with tact and patience). And my writing group, The Coven, who hold my hand (both metaphorically and literally), talk me down off the ledge when things get crazy and generally keep me sane. I love you, girls!

Also, a separate special thanks goes to Kitty and her friend Betsy for answering my questions on what it takes to be a teacher in the States.

* * *

The Highest Bidder
*At this high-stakes auction house,
where everything is for sale,
true love is priceless.*

Don't miss a single story in this new continuity
from Harlequin Desire!

One

"Five hundred thousand. I have half a million dollars, ladies and gentlemen. Any more bids?"

The auctioneer's French-accented baritone rose above the electric whispers spreading through the eager crowd at Waverly's. The atmosphere was a living, breathing thing, undulating in intense waves of excitement and curiosity, and Chase Harrington could practically feel the energy bouncing off each and every bidder in the room, the familiar subdued rumble of gossip reverberating off the velvet-papered walls.

The chandeliered auction room with its tufted high-backed chairs and polished wooden floor was a far cry from Obscure, Texas. And for once, no one was gossiping about him: they were all fixated on the auction.

Being able to offer D. B. Dunbar's hand-notated final draft for sale had been a massive coup for Waverly's, one of New York's oldest—and most scandalous—auction houses. Millions around the world had been riveted by the tragic death of America's famous children's author in a plane crash last October. But after the usual outpouring of grief, commentary quickly turned to the issue of the reclusive thirty-year-old's final book in his acclaimed Charlie Jack: Teenage Ninja Warrior series. Countless Facebook fan pages, regular trending on Twitter and fan fiction sites were all about one thing—was there a fourth book and, if so, when would it be published?

Now, *that* was full-scale attention.

Chase's fingers tightened on his paddle, nerves as tight as a teenager on his first date. Enter the distant relative, some cousin twice removed, desperate for money and fame.. Walter...Walter...Shalvey, that was it. Yeah, Shalvey was a narcissistic bottom feeder, but unfortunately he knew how to play the media, drip-feeding just enough information to keep the story in the public eye for months. The guy was not only set for life, thanks to lucrative royalties and associated licensing fees from the first three books. There was also a fourth book—Dunbar's agent had just sold it for seven figures last week, with a scheduled publication date of April.

Which was way too late.

Chase cast an impatient glance over the crowded room. Judging by the turnout today, the hype had worked. Not that it was any old public auction, oh, no. Invitation only meant handpicked rich, famous or otherwise connected. He'd already spotted a politician and a socialite, plus an incognito actor who was rumored to be interested in the movie rights for his production company.

The extremely private Dunbar would probably be rolling over in his grave right about now.

"Any more bids?" repeated the auctioneer, his gavel poised and ready to call the sale.

Chase may have spent years honing his "detached and aloof" expression, but inside, a triumphant smile itched to escape. That manuscript would be his. He could almost taste it.

"Five hundred and *ten* thousand dollars. Thank you, ma'am."

A unified gasp coursed through the crowd, drowning out Chase's soft curse. Fist clenched tight on his paddle, he smoothly lifted it.

The auctioneer nodded at him. "Five hundred and twenty."

The sharply dressed blonde sitting next to him finally looked up from her cell phone. "You *do* know the book is being published in six months, right?"

"Yes."

She paused, but when Chase said no more, shrugged and went back to her phone.

Another wave of murmurs bathed the spectators, then... "Five hundred and thirty thousand dollars."

Oh, no, you don't. Chase raised his paddle again then followed the auctioneer's gaze.

His rival was on the far side of the room, three rows up, standing with her back against the wall. Petite, huge eyes, fiery-red hair pulled back into a no-nonsense hairdo, grim expression. He noticed all that within seconds then, oddly, *that severe black suit isn't working with her pale skin.*

Right. But she *was* determined, judging by the way she countered his bid again, her brows dipping before her chin tipped up defiantly.

She was also, he realized as he ruthlessly picked her apart, a woman totally focused on projecting a haughty, untouchable facade. A woman obviously used to getting her own way.

And just like that, a broken fragment of his past jabbed him, flattening his mouth as a thousand sour memories filled it.

Oh, no. You are not sixteen anymore and she is definitely not a Perfect.

The Perfects... Man, he'd managed to not think about those three jerks and their catty girlfriends in years. Perfect in looks, perfect in social skills, perfect in freezing out anyone labeled "unsuitable" by their beautiful standards. Goddamn Perfects had made high school a living hell. He'd barely gotten out alive.

He glared at the woman, cataloging the familiar arrogant tilt of her chin, the aura of entitlement and control, the superiority as she looked down her nose at everyone. Judging him, finding him lacking. Unacceptable. Unworthy.

Get it together, man. You buried that life a thousand times over. You're not that helpless boy with the white-trash parents anymore.

Yet he couldn't take his eyes off her. His teeth ground together so tightly his jaw began to ache.

He finally tore his gaze back to the auctioneer before the poison filled him, and called out loudly, "One million dollars."

The ripple of surprise erupted into a tsunami. Chase glanced over at his rival, his face expressionless. *Try beating that, princess.*

She blinked once, twice, those huge eyes studying him with such silent intent that he felt a frown furrow his brow.

Then she turned away, her paddle loose at her side as she shook her head at the auctioneer.

It was over a few seconds later.

Yes. Victory pulsed through him as he stood and made his way down the row of congratulatory observers.

"Congratulations," the blonde said as she followed him through the tightly packed crowd. "Me, I could think of better things to spend a million bucks on."

Chase gave her a thin smile then glanced across the room one last time.

She was gone.

He scanned the crowd. Blonde. Blonde. Brunette. Not red enough. Ah…

His gaze lingered and people began to move, finally parting to offer a better view.

She was talking to a tall blonde woman in a sharp suit, and as that woman turned, recognition hit.

Ann Richardson, beleaguered CEO of Waverly's.

He'd read more than he cared to about Waverly's these past months. Movie stars, scandals, a missing golden statue. Crazy stuff that belonged in bestselling fiction, not real life. Sometimes he found it hard to believe he actually moved in some of the same social circles.

But he knew firsthand how dark the flipside could be, especially when money was involved. Take Ann Richardson—a driven, charismatic woman who'd dragged the Waverly name through the tabloids, thanks to her alleged affair with Dalton Rothschild.

He scowled. There was something about Rothschild that rubbed him the wrong way... Oh, he had bags of charm and was a talented businessman, but Chase had never liked the way he seemed to seek the spotlight for every charity event, every donation he made. Too overdone, Chase had always thought.

While he suffered a few more handshakes, his gaze returned to the two women, noting the familiar way they chatted, the hand Ann placed on the redhead's arm, the smiles. Then they bent their heads and a quick volley of words flew, in between a few surreptitious looks that could only mean they were exchanging something private.

A sliver of doubt took hold.

Chase pulled out his phone and on the pretext of checking his calls, studied the women more closely.

To a casual observer, the redhead's appearance was impeccable. But Chase was looking for flaws and pretty soon his keen eyes found them. A loose thread on her cuff, sharp creases on her jacket—both pointed to lots of wardrobe storage. Then there was her bag, which showed faint wear along the leather handles.

He hesitated at her legs, appreciating the lean calves for a moment until he dragged his gaze down. Impossibly high shoes, shiny and obviously expensive. And vaguely familiar.

His thoughtful frown cleared. Yeah, that fashion designer he'd dated a few years back had had a thing for shoes and she'd had the exact same style in five different colors. If these were real, they were at least three years old. If they were fake, it only created more questions.

The redhead slowly shifted her weight from one leg to the other and winced, a dead giveaway that her feet were killing her. So, a woman not used to wearing fancy shoes. A woman— he quickly realized—who definitely did not have half a million to spare.

All those little anomalies exploded into full-blown suspicion. He'd seen more than his fair share of underhand deals not to realize something was off.

Anger flared, making his gut tighten. Coincidence? No way. Things always happened for a reason, not because of some cosmic karma. The redhead was up to something. Her conflicting appearance, her link to Ann Richardson, combined with Richardson's tainted reputation…

Anger and distaste swelled up inside. If Richardson had resorted to shill bidding then Chase was *not* going to let her get away with it.

Lost, lost, lost. Vanessa's red-heeled Louboutins tattooed out that one word as she clacked down Waverly's polished hall, her throat thick with disappointment.

Her failure had been briefly overshadowed by seeing Ann Richardson, her sister's college roommate, and for a few minutes she was simply Juliet's sister, exchanging friendly chatter and playing catch-up.

"Juliet's in Washington for a few weeks, you know," Vanessa had said. "You should give her a call and we could do lunch sometime. That is," she amended, belatedly recalling the recent sensational headlines, "if you're not too busy."

Ann smiled. "I'm always busy. But it is tempting. A chance to get away from the city would be welcome."

Vanessa knew how she felt.

They chatted about the auction for a few minutes, then Vanessa's family, until she regretfully mentioned her flight and Ann offered the use of her car. She wanted to refuse, but the truth was a chauffeured ride would provide more privacy than a New York cabdriver.

Privacy to wallow in her failure.

Gone, gone, gone, her heels continued to tap out on the white marbled floor.

She'd bid as high as she could, but her grandmother's considerable trust fund just wasn't enough. *Sorry, Meme.* She sighed as she tied her coat belt with a swift tug. *I know you'd think I was crazy for wanting something from that man. But you always said a family legacy was one of the most important gifts you can give your children.*

And all she'd gotten for her trouble was a bunch of aching muscles from pulling her shoulders straight, a painful reward for donning that familiar air of cool world-weariness designed to keep any curious onlookers at bay.

She kept up the brisk pace, her face still tight as she passed by an ornate mirror.

It had been so long since she'd needed her game face, but old ways died hard. *Well, of course they did. It's been drummed into you since you were five years old.* And for twenty-two more she'd lived it with outward acceptance. "You are a Partridge," was her father's favorite lecture. "Your forefathers were one of the founding families of this great city of Washington. You do not show weakness or vulnerability and you never, ever do anything to taint the noble legacy of those ancestors."

She grabbed the door handle as emotion tumbled inside. Well, she'd well and truly tainted that legacy; she'd not only thrown away a career in law for a teaching degree, then quit the position her father had arranged at the exclusively private Winchester Prep: she'd ended up unwed and pregnant. In the eyes of the great Allen Partridge, that was a bigger offense than her teaching job at Bright Stars Nursery School. She'd felt his scorn and disappointment for days under his roof until she'd finally decided to move.

"Excuse me." A large male hand suddenly slapped on the door, shoving it closed and breaking her thoughts.

"What do you think you're…?" She whirled, but the rest of her sentence petered off as she stared up into a pair of angry blue eyes. *Nice face. Very nice face. No, wait!* It was Mr. Million Dollars, the smug suit who'd won what should have been hers. "…doing?" she finished in irritation.

She put her weight on the back foot, creating distance even as her fingers tightened on her handbag.

Animosity seeped from every pore of his sharply dressed body, broad shoulders straight, cool arrogance lining an impressively striking face. Tanned skin, chiseled jaw. Her inner artist paused to admire the view. Classically handsome, really…

"Who are you?" he barked.

She blinked, the spell broken. "None of your business. Who are *you?*"

"Someone who can make a lot of trouble for you. How do you know Ann Richardson?"

Vanessa shoved her handbag strap up her shoulder. "Again, none of your business. Now, if you'll excuse me?"

The man refused to budge, preferring instead to stare her down.

Yeah, good luck with that, buddy.

She raised one condescending eyebrow then slowly crossed her arms. "Do I need to call security?"

"Oh, go right ahead. I'm sure they'll be interested in your story."

What? Confusion spiked, followed quickly by a thread of worry. She drew in a sharp breath. "Look, I don't know who you think I am or what I've—"

He snorted. "Cut the crap. I know exactly what you've been doing. The question is, do you want to come clean or should I do it for you?"

The cold steel in his voice matched his eyes, slicing through her tough protective shell in one swift movement.

"Come clean?" she said faintly.

"Yeah. And I'm sure I could wrangle a few reporters interested enough to run a story."

Shock stole her voice, her breath. *How could he know? No one knew.* Her hand flew to her throat, her fingers tightening around her woolen collar.

Yet as he stood there, bristling and combative as he invaded her personal space, a thought began to grow inside, pushing past her outrage and fear. What was it her father always said? "Until there's irrefutable evidence, never admit to anything."

Wow, it did help to have a defense lawyer in the family.

A shot of resolve forced her hand into a tight fist by her side. Quickly she called on every tired muscle to straighten her already ramrod back as she inhaled, filling her lungs with self-assurance.

"And what story would that be?" she said calmly, pinning him with her direct gaze.

His murmur of disbelief annoyed the hell out of her. "Shill bidding."

She blinked. "What?"

"A plant, bidding against—"

"Legitimate bidders to bump up the price. Yes, I know what it is. And you… you—" she released a relieved breath "—are out of your mind."

"Are you denying you know Ann Richardson?"

Vanessa's mouth tightened. "Of course I know her—she was my sister's college roommate."

The stranger's expression turned shrewd. "Right." His gaze swept over her, scrutinizing, studying. Frankly contemptuous in his perusal.

That faint sheen of worry started up again, sending a shiver down her spine. *Careful, Ness.* "It's true, and very easily proved."

"Of course it is."

"Listen, Mr.…?"

"Harrington. Chase Harrington."

"Mr. Harrington. You won the auction. You are now the proud owner of the rare and precious hand-notated copy of D. B. Dunbar's final book—" Her voice nearly cracked then, but she swallowed and forged on. "So go and pay Waverly's and enjoy your prize. Now, if you'll excuse me…"

"So why were you bidding on Dunbar's manuscript?"

She dug around in her bag for her sunglasses. "Why did everyone else in that room want it?"

"I'm asking you, not them."

With a deliberately bored shrug, she slid her glasses on. "I hate waiting. Especially for a D. B. Dunbar."

He crossed his arms, his expression part skeptical, part disgusted. "You couldn't wait six months."

"That's right."

"Bull."

The stress of the past few years, the tense auction, missing her babies and the frantic craziness of New York had done their damage, steadily chipping away at her control. And now this... this... arrogant SOB in her face. She'd had enough.

Resentment surged through her veins, heating her face and pulling her shoulders back. She shoved her glasses on her head then tipped her chin up, giving him her haughtiest death stare.

"You know what? You got me. You want to know who I am?" When she took an aggressive step forward, surprise flashed across his face, and empowered, she took another. "I was Dunbar's secret girlfriend, he left me with nothing and I was bidding on that manuscript so I could wait a few months, then flog it off for a nice little profit when his book came out. That sound about right to you?"

She punctuated every word with a pointing finger, until finally she paused, a bare inch away from poking that finger into his broad chest.

His eyes were a sharp, clear blue, the kind of blue reserved for movie stars and rock gods. Yet strangely, it reminded her of a perfect Colorado winter, the morning after the first snowfall.

Contact lenses, probably. His whole persona screamed money and entitlement, and with that, ego and vanity came hand in hand. Yet as she paused, breath pumping from her lungs and fists now on hips, his gaze flicked to her mouth.

The moment flared, so sudden and intense that Vanessa sucked in a gasp. Her anger shorted out as awareness flooded in, infinite possibilities and anticipation threading through the air, binding them.

It left her reeling.

Chase couldn't help but notice how wide those green eyes had become. Innocent eyes, he would've said, if not for the fact that she'd spent the last twenty seconds practically screaming her crazy scenario at him.

And boy, a woman with a mouth *that* good was as far from innocent as he was.

He dragged in a breath, then quickly exhaled when he realized it was all her. Something vanilla, plus something else… soft and powdery, familiar yet unable to place.

Princess smelled amazing, and that pissed him off because the last thing he needed was a raging attraction to *her*. He couldn't. He *wouldn't*. He didn't do commitment or Perfects.

Control. He had to get control.

"Miss Partridge?" came a voice, and as one, they both sprung back and turned.

A uniformed man stood there, a cap tucked under his arm.

"Yes?" she said, her chin going up, eyebrows raised in an imperious "why are you interrupting me" expression.

"Miss Richardson said to inform you her car is ready for you. Where would you like to go?"

She spared Chase a haughty look. "JFK, thanks." And without another word, she turned on her heel and followed the driver down the long corridor.

She had the rounded tones and patrician air that clenched every muscle in Chase's body, sending it onto high alert. She even had the walk down pat, he realized, watching her hips sway beneath that tight black skirt, her precise footsteps in killer heels eating up the hall. Part hypnotic, part infuriating, that arrogant walk told him she knew exactly where his eyes were focused. He'd bet a thousand bucks a smug smile was plastered all over that beautiful face, too.

With hands on his hips he glared at her back until she turned the corner and finally disappeared.

She hadn't declared her innocence or answered his questions. And now he had a name—Partridge. Which meant this was far from over.

Two

Chase checked his watch for the fifth time in as many minutes then stared out into the dark, leafy suburban street, shifting restlessly in the luxurious leather seat of his rental car as his thoughts tossed.

Vanessa Partridge. His gaze honed in on the apartment building three doors down, at the lights behind the drawn curtains on the second floor.

At first he'd thought there was something in that manuscript, something incriminating she wanted to remain private. But apart from a stack of hand-written notes and a bunch of chapters running low on toner, he'd come up empty.

He'd stared at those neat pages on his desk for so long he could've burned a hole in them. And eventually he returned to his original accusation—she was a Waverly plant.

He buttoned up his coat then swung open the car door, wincing as an unseasonably cold October breeze rushed in. A thousand questions burned, their missing endings gnawing away at him. Despite the information Chase had charmed out of Waverly's staff, then had followed up online, nothing could fill in the gaps better than the woman herself. Yes, her story about her sister and Ann Richardson had proven correct, but the rest was woefully deficient…and he hated the imperfection those holes wrought.

Why would Vanessa Partridge resort to shill bidding? And why would the daughter of two highly respected Washington lawyers have such a blatant disregard for the law?

Chase shoved his hands in his pockets. If she was as innocent as she claimed, how could she afford to bid on that manuscript, given her single-parent status and teacher's salary? Daddy's money? So why not use that money for a house, a flashy car, a nanny?

Those questions had dogged his thoughts after he'd observed her leaving the nursery school where she worked, dressed in jeans and a battered bomber jacket, hair tied in a simple ponytail. He'd watched in fascination as she went through what was obviously the familiar process of carrying two babies outside, strapping them into her old BMW, throwing her bags into the trunk, then driving fifteen minutes to a double-story apartment block. One of many that lined an average street in the lower end of Silver Spring, Maryland.

Everything about Vanessa Partridge screamed respectability, from her old-money Washington-lawyer parents, to her centuries-old bloodline. But she also baffled him. Why would someone turn her back on a promising career in law, one where she could fall into the family practice straight after her bar exam? When he'd read that particular bit of information he'd known that a trip to Maryland was in the cards. He dealt in speculation every single waking moment: it's what he did, first as the new guy at Rushford Investments, then as one of McCoy Jameson's most sought-after portfolio managers. These days, he worked for himself and a few choice investors. He had a talent for making money and he'd made an obscene amount of it over the years, even through the turbulent time following the crash. He was pretty much free to please himself.

And right now, what pleased him was figuring out the puzzle that was Vanessa Partridge because everything about her just didn't add up.

He stared up at the drawn curtains of Vanessa's apartment.

If it somehow turned out he was wrong, he owed her an apology. Chase Harrington always admitted his mistakes. But the only way he'd get to the truth was by confronting her.

No, not confronting. He'd done that back in New York and look what had happened—she'd been all up in his face and then, *wham!* That moment when he'd suddenly felt the inexplicable urge to kiss her.

His breath puffed out, clouding in the cool night air. Dammit. She was a Perfect in every sense of the word, and not just by the standards of his narrow-minded hometown. She had the breeding, the money, the attitude…the looks. That skin, the hair. The mouth—that beautifully shaped, top-heavy mouth, coupled with those wide green eyes…

With a muffled curse he slammed his car door closed. *Get a grip, Chase.* He'd fought hard to keep his past in the past, even though it had molded him into the man he was today, guiding his decisions so he could get as far away as possible from his previous life. Far away from people like Vanessa Partridge.

She'd piqued his curiosity and raised too many flags. If she was a shill bidder, he had to report her.

And if she wasn't?

His mind flashed back to earlier, when he'd watched her struggle to get her two children into the car.

Until he knew what her story was and how she was connected to his manuscript, he needed a cool head. Angry meant emotional, and *that* had the potential for mistakes. He'd learned that lesson from a very early age.

"Good girl, Heather. You ate all your dinner!" Vanessa gently wiped the drooly, smiling mouth of her eighteen-month-old daughter before turning to the little girl's twin, who sat beside her in an identical high chair. "And how are you doing, Erin? Still painting?"

The chocolate-curled baby looked up from her pumpkin-smeared tray to grin. "Pain!" Then she slowly stuck her fingers in her mouth, her eyes twinkling in mischief.

Vanessa laughed, swiping away a fleck of food in the toddler's hair. "That's some mighty fine artwork you've got there. Edible, too. How avant-garde of you."

Wanting in on the conversation, Heather clapped her hands and squealed, prompting her sister to follow suit. Pumpkin splattered Vanessa's shirt, leaving orange smears on dark blue. Vanessa quickly wiped it off with a smile, even as her insides cramped with bittersweet regret.

She'd been back home for two days, back to her normal life and her job and still she couldn't shake the failure of her New York trip.

I am very disappointed in you, Vanessa. If she closed her eyes, that imaginary voice even sounded like her father's.

She cupped Heather's warm cheek with her palm, her mouth grim.

Yes, she had friends, her girls, a job she loved. All those had satisfied her for nearly two years. A few times she'd thought of calling her parents, even apologizing, but she quickly nixed that idea. *She* had nothing to apologize *for*.

Then she'd heard about the auction and it was as if she'd been hit by a renewed purpose. Something had taken hold of her conscience and wouldn't let go, a righteous emotion that had amplified day by day, night by night, until two weeks ago. She'd thought about it, analyzed it to death before allowing herself to hope, to plan, to follow up. Dylan may have left her—left her babies—with nothing to remember him by, but she was determined to right that wrong.

She'd failed.

Obviously, someone up there didn't want her to have that manuscript.

She sighed, gently wiping pumpkin from Heather's high chair. So many memories rolling through her head. So many mistakes.

Well, except two. Her gaze went to Erin and Heather, glee-fully mucking about with their food, and her chest tightened to almost painful intensity. She'd go through her father's hor-rible accusations, their awful row and her storming out all over again if it meant having these two gorgeous babies in her life. They were hers. All hers.

"Mum-mum-mum?" Heather said, huge brown eyes so like Dylan's staring up at her.

Vanessa's breath caught as she leaned in to kiss the soft, downy head. Lingering notes of baby shampoo mixed with pumpkin quickly chased away the regret and she smiled.

"I think it's time for someone's bath."

"Baff!" Erin echoed with a final bang on her high chair.

With smooth efficiency, she wiped down the high chairs then unstrapped the girls. With one on each hip, she padded out of the kitchen, through the living room and down the short hall.

This apartment was perfect, although sharing her master bath would definitely lose its appeal once the girls got older. Eventually they'd have to find a bigger place, something with three bedrooms and at least two bathrooms.

Maybe fate was telling her she needed to use her money for more important things.

Shoving all thoughts of that auction from her mind, she concentrated on the familiar routine of bathing the girls, dry-ing them, reading a bedtime story, then settling them down in their cribs. As usual, Erin was the first to fall asleep, her little breath coming in deep and even almost immediately. Heather was the restless one, unable to settle unless Vanessa was softly singing, her hand a reassuring pressure on her back.

She was halfway through the second song of her nightly Rascal Flatts repertoire when Heather finally stilled and her breathing changed.

With a soft sigh, Vanessa gently drew her hand away, tip-toed across the room and pulled the door to.

She was nearly to the kitchen when the phone rang.

She surged forward and grabbed the receiver off the wall. "Hello?"

"Evening, Vanessa. It's Connor Jarvis from number fifteen."

Her heart sank. Her elderly neighbor took his self-designated role as McKenzie Road's protector of the street's females seriously. While it was flattering most of the time, tonight was not the night. "Hi, Mr. Jarvis. What can I do for you?"

"Well, I know the Taylors below you are away for the month and, ahhh…" She waited patiently for Jarvis's hacking cough to subside. Finally he wheezed, "So you know I told you about that guy loitering at number seven last night?"

"Yes?"

"Well, I don't want to alarm you, but I think he's out in front of your place."

"What?"

She walked swiftly over to the living room window, dipping down the blinds a bare inch and staring at the lamp-lit street.

"Outside?" she said. "Where?"

"He was at the curb a few minutes ago, looking up at your window. But now I can't see him." Jarvis paused again, coughing for long-drawn-out seconds.

"You sure it was a man?" Vanessa said, slowly scanning the shadows outside.

"Couldn't miss it. Tall, broad. Dressed in a suit, for crying out loud. What kind of criminal wears a suit?"

"Ones who're good at their job?"

Jarvis burst into wheezy laughter until Vanessa began to feel bad about her lame joke. Finally, he got it under control enough to say, "You want me to call the cops?"

Before she could answer, she caught movement in her yard. The security light came on a second later, bathing the would-be criminal in a harsh amber glow.

Vanessa sucked in a breath as her stomach bottomed out.

"You want me to call the cops?" Jarvis repeated.

"No. No, I…" She sighed. "I know him. Thanks for letting me know, Mr. Jarvis. I'll deal with it. You have a good night."

She quickly hung up before the man had a chance to grill her further.

Vanessa paused in the middle of her living room, moments passing before she realized she had the tip of her thumb in her mouth, the nail flicking back and forth over her front tooth.

Fingers out of your mouth, Vanessa!

She winced. Even now, the mere memory of her father's commanding bellow still had the power to make her jump.

Focus. Chase Harrington. Right.

She *could* ignore him.

Yeah, right. You think Mr. Million Dollars would stand for being ignored?

Her mind whirled with too many questions lacking answers. What on earth was he doing here? Lord, had he actually thought she'd been serious about her sarcastic Dylan's "girlfriend" crack? So what did he want? She swallowed. And the big one—did he know about the girls?

She hesitated, uncertain and unprepared until the doorbell made the decision for her. In a flurry of irritation she raced down the steps and yanked the door open.

"Don't touch that bell again!"

His hand hovered, then dropped as he stared at her through the security screen. He dominated the space on her porch—tall, broad-shouldered and dressed in an expensive suit, an equally fine winter coat only emphasizing his impressive frame. "Okay."

"Are you stalking me, Mr. Harrington?" She crossed her arms against the night chill.

"No. I just want to talk to you."

"If you've tracked me down to accuse me of something else—"

"That's not it." He shoved his hands in his pockets. "Can we talk inside?"

"You could be a psychopath for all I know," she retorted. Of course, she'd checked up on Mr. Million Dollars—*have to stop calling him that!*—days ago. And what she'd found gave no indication he was a criminal…at least, not on the record, anyway.

Across the street a light came on—Connor Jarvis's—and she sighed. After a quick glance up the stairs, she unlatched the screen door. "Fine. Come in."

He paused on the threshold. "I could be a psychopath."

"Apparently you're not, or so Google says."

Surprise flashed across his face and she swallowed a satisfied smile, adding, "Silver Spring's a bit far from One Madison Park just for a talk."

Yes, I've been checking up on you. She let him digest that as she relatched the door.

She hadn't forgotten their encounter, least of all that weird, tense moment just before Ann's driver had inadvertently rescued her. She'd spent the last few days trying to forget it, steadfastly refusing to do what she normally did, which was scrutinize every single word, every action and reaction, then sort and define subtext and body language, keeping herself awake at night in the process.

She could practically hear her sister Juliet's teasing laughter ringing in her ears. *You always analyze things way too much, Ness. Does he like me? Do I like him? Should I hold his hand? Should I kiss him? And if I do, will it mean I'm too easy?*

She'd interpreted Dylan's interest—correctly, as it turned out—and followed up on it, which was how she'd ended up in his bed. And boy, had *that* turned out to be one colossal misjudgment on her part.

Only an idiot makes the same mistake twice, chère, her grandma used to say. *And Partridges are smarter than that.*

She finally turned to face him, the hall's subdued lighting creating shadows and slashes of light across his face. Unfortunately, it was a very nice face and Vanessa could feel the unwanted flicker of attraction warm her insides.

He's just a good-looking guy. Yet there was something else, something behind those carefully shuttered eyes, that called to her, something different.

Yeah, you always go for the brooding, intelligent, emotionally stunted ones, don't you?

Vanessa clamped down hard on all emotion, instead letting righteous indignation flow freely. Chase Harrington here, in her home, did not bode well, of that she was certain.

Three

"Look, you've obviously been checking up on me, Mr. Harrington," she began, arms crossed and eyes hard. "So you should know I was a legitimate bidder in that auction."

"It's Chase."

Chase studied her as she stared at him expectantly, her legs planted wide and arms crossed in a classic defensive stance.

Chase tipped his head. "You're swaying."

Her cheeks flushed and she abruptly stilled. "Force of habit. So...you were telling me why you were here."

Good question he'd yet to fully answer himself. Did rampant curiosity count or would that make him really sound like a stalker? "What you said at Waverly's—the bit about you being Dunbar's girlfriend. Was it true?"

She blinked, shock leaking out before she swiftly wiped her expression clean. "No. And anyway, what possible interest is my life to someone like—" she put her hand out, palm up, and swept him from head to toe "—you?"

That got his back up. "What's that supposed to mean?"

"What?"

"That little…" He mimicked her gesture with a lot less finesse.

She pulled her back straight, chin tipping up. "I mean, you are obviously a rich man. Someone with connections and power and influence…"—*did she just curl her lip?*—"And I, on the other hand, am not."

"Oh, I wouldn't sell yourself short, Miss Partridge."

She frowned and there was that look again, that irritating-as-all-hell flash of arrogance. It was an expression so effortlessly executed he wondered if she'd spent hours practicing in the mirror.

Chase gritted his teeth. *Yeah, this was such a great idea.*

As they silently glared at each other, a baby's muffled cry drifted down the stairs, cutting through the charged air. Vanessa's gaze snapped away, then she put a foot on the first step. "If that's all you came to say…?"

"There's more."

Irritation flared in those wide green eyes, but she reined it in with practiced ease.

"Go," he said, nodding up the stairs. "I'll wait."

With a frown and a grudging "fine," she turned away.

Chase's gaze followed her jeans-clad bottom as it swayed upward, one mesmerizing step at a time. In fact, he couldn't tear his eyes away. Bare feet… Nicely filled pair of denims…

Wait, what?

He shook his head then dug fingernails into his clenched palm for good measure. Blood pounded in his ears, drowning out her rapid steps.

He'd managed to gain control when she returned fifteen minutes later, her hands brushing back a few stray hairs as she slowly descended.

"You have a baby," he stated, feigning ignorance.

She crossed her arms. "Two girls. Twins. But considering you know where I live, I'm pretty sure you already know that." When he slowly nodded, she narrowed her eyes. "Why the interest in me?"

"Why did you want Dunbar's manuscript?"

"I told you why." She cocked her hip, hands going to her waist as she effected a deliberately bored expression. "I hate waiting."

Chase sighed. She was trying too hard and his patience was dwindling. But instead of plowing through her facade, he moved on. "So you're a D. B. Dunbar fan."

"Of his books, yes."

He swiftly picked up on that correction with no outward indication. What did she think he'd meant?

Then she added, "So you must be quite a fan too."

"Me? No."

She frowned. "You've never read any of his books?" At his head shake, she said incredulously, *"Charlie Jack? Calm Before the Storm? Justice Prevailed?"*

"No."

"You should. He is...*was*..." She paused, searching for the rights words before settling on, "Incredibly, amazingly talented. The world he painted just takes you to another place." She smiled the smile of a true believer. "There are a finite number of words in the English language, yet when D. B. Dunbar arranged them he did it in such a way every page just sang. He was—" she hesitated a brief second, a flash of something behind her eyes "—a great writer."

He'd bet a thousand bucks that wasn't what she was originally going to say.

She brushed her hair back again, the other hand going to her back pocket. "So why did you buy the manuscript if you're not a fan?"

"It's a collector's item," he said neutrally. "A good investment that will only increase in value with the author dead."

A flinch. Just a small one, barely noticeable. But he still caught it.

A thread of disquiet surged.

In New York she'd been as slick and icy as a January sidewalk. But here, on her own turf, not so Perfect. That is, if you didn't count that haughty display earlier.

"You didn't answer my question," she said, recrossing her arms. "Why the interest in me?"

"Because I wanted to make sure you were on the level. And if you were, I owed you an apology."

Her brow twisted into confusion. "A phone call would've sufficed."

"Ah, but you could've hung up on me."

"Most probably. So, Mr. Harrington—" she crossed her arms "—what did you find out about me?"

Oh, boy. Amazingly, he found himself tongue-tied, trapped beneath that challenging green gaze like a fifteen-year-old kid caught spying on the girls' bathroom. He took a steadying breath, unable to shake the remnants of his past. "Your sister and Ann did go to college, your parents are hugely successful lawyers. You started out studying law but instead changed your major. But…"

"But what?" She lifted her brow questioningly. "You've come all this way, you might as well ask. Whether I'll answer, though, is another thing."

"You're not exactly flush with cash, are you?"

"How could I afford to bid, you mean?" Her face tightened, shoulders straightening. "I have an inheritance from my maternal grandmother."

Oh, this just gets better. Of course Vanessa Partridge has an inheritance. "But not enough to outbid me."

Her mouth thinned. "No."

Chase's outward expression revealed nothing of the confusion warring inside. Her response didn't feel rehearsed, and he'd seen some standout performances in his time. So, if he scratched shill bidder, what was left? She was more than just a rabid fan.

But how to approach it so she wouldn't end up kicking him out?

Fresh out of inspiration, he glanced up at her brightly painted blue door. "So, what are your girls' names?"

She hesitated then said slowly, "Erin and Heather."

Chase's eyebrows shot up. *Score.* "The characters in Dunbar's manuscript."

"What?"

She grabbed the stair railing, her eyes rounding.

He put out a steadying hand, but she waved it away with an "are you kidding me?" look. Suitably chastened, he watched her shake her head, her gaze on the floor.

"I skimmed through the manuscript," he continued slowly. Her thick auburn ponytail slid over her shoulder as her chin dipped and she placed one hand on her hip. "About halfway in he introduces two characters called Megan and Tori. But in his notes, he renames them."

Her head snapped up. "Did the notes explain why?"

"No."

"So the published version will be—"

"Heather and Erin. Your daughters." He paused, then added calmly, "And Dunbar's."

Silence fell, stretching interminably, punctuated only by the thick exhale of her breath. Shock? Anger? A prelude to tears? Whatever was going through her head, he knew one thing with unerring certainty: Vanessa Partridge wasn't the type to cry in public. Her straightened shoulders and lifted chin just seconds later proved that thought.

"You'd better come up."

His brow lifted. "You sure?"

With a swift nod, she turned and went back up the stairs.

Refusing to focus on her rear end, Chase finally reached the top and followed her inside. He took in the short horizontal hallway and a glimpse of a bedroom to the right before she pointed in the opposite direction and said, "Take a seat."

He did as she asked and walked into her living room.

Stacks of books, their spines creased and worn, lined the far wall of the cozy room, spreading out under the large window to his left, before a small television and DVD player filled the remaining gap. A high shelf housed a multitude of keepsakes—a candle holder, an oddly-shaped clay sculpture and a dozen tiny origami figures. Magazines cluttered the coffee table, along with a stack of colored paper and a jar of chunky crayons. A playpen sat center, bracketed by a corner lounge chair.

So, was this the real Vanessa Partridge?

He gave her apartment another once-over. Why would someone with silver-spoon parents be living in a rental and working as an underpaid preschool teacher?

Vanessa closed the door behind them, her mind a whirling mass of chaos and confusion. Why? Why had Dylan…?

That phone call.

"I have to talk to you." That was it. One scratchy, tinny message he'd left on her voice mail. She'd assumed he'd meant "right away" and gone from hopefully optimistic to raging fury after three hours and five messages and he still hadn't shown up. Then she'd turned on the TV and discovered Dylan was not only half a world away, but he'd died in a plane crash.

She slowly walked into her living room. Never had she felt the sting of bewilderment so keenly than at this exact moment. Yes, she'd been dumb enough to get involved with a guy incapable of loving her the way she should be loved, and that awful, gut-gouging hope when she'd played his last message over and over had been her own personal torture device for days.

But this? This was off the charts.

She'd had no one to confide in after the accident, which had magnified her isolation a thousandfold. When the news had run the D.B. Dunbar stories 24/7 for weeks, interviewing his neighbors, his editor, his assistant, all she could do was stare at the screen with a mix of frustration and anger. Starting her new life and new job had been hard, but they'd been minor traumas compared to the ever-constant ripples that being D. B. Dunbar's secret girlfriend had wrought.

And Chase Harrington was the only other person alive who knew the truth.

Well, more than most. She shot him a panicky glance.

"So what—" she began.

A soft muffle interrupted them and their eyes met. Vanessa turned and started down the hall until Chase's hand on her wrist pulled her up short.

"Wait." She stared at him, then at his warm fingers encircling her wrist. He let her go. "Just talk to her from outside the door. Don't go in there and don't turn on any lights."

She frowned. "Why…"

The cries grew louder and Chase added, "Can you just try it?"

Vanessa glared at him then silently went down the hall to the door slightly ajar. "It's okay, Heather," she began softly.

"Higher. More singsongy."

Of all the— She gritted her teeth and did as he instructed. "Mommy's heeeere. Just go back to sleep, sweetie."

She paused, letting Heather mutter again before adding gently, "Time for sleepy, sweetie. Baaaaaack tooooo sleeeeeep."

She held her breath, waiting. After a second or two of baby mumbles, silence fell.

No. Way. She slowly turned to Chase, staring at him incredulously. "How did you know that?"

He shrugged. "I spent a lot of time with kids when I was younger. It seemed to work for them."

When a sudden wail pierced the air, Chase added wryly, "But obviously not for Heather."

Vanessa shot Chase a look then went swiftly into the girls' room. The soft glow of the night-light spread across the walls and ceiling, highlighting Heather in the cot, flat on her back with eyes screwed up, ready to throw herself into her usual crying jag. Vanessa began the routine: a low gentle croon, slowly flipping her to her side, then rubbing her back, all the while scanning the mattress then the pillow.

Aha! She grabbed the pacifier and wrapped Heather's fingers around the plastic handle. Almost instantly, Heather shoved the rubber nipple in her mouth and started to grumble, sucking furiously.

So very angry. Vanessa smiled. Erin couldn't care less, she was so laid-back. But Heather—her fierce little warrior girl—couldn't sleep without one.

With a quick check on the still-sound-asleep Erin, Vanessa made a silent exit, shaking her head as she padded back to the living room.

Chase was standing in the middle of her space, hands behind his back and legs apart. It was such a typically male stance, one that indicated control and command, that she felt her defenses go on full alert.

"Heather only wakes up when she loses her pacifier," she said, trying to ignore the authority he radiated.

"Ahhh."

"Erin could sleep through a bomb blast."

He gave her a wry smile and for just one second, Vanessa wondered what it'd be like if he put everything into it. Devastating, most probably.

"You have kids?" she began.

"No. Look, I should apologize and—"

"Would you like a—" she said simultaneously. They both stopped, waited a second, then started again.

"...go."

"...drink?"

Again, silence descended, but this time, Chase's mouth curved and suddenly all Vanessa could hear was her heartbeat as it picked up the pace.

Mr. Million-Dollar Smile. Wow.

"I—I have coffee," she said faintly, hating the way she stumbled over those three simple words. She quickly attempted to drag back the tattered remnants of composure, but his smile told her she was fooling no one with her straight back and square shoulders.

In fact, that smile only brought out a dimple. A dimple, for heaven's sakes! As if he didn't have enough money and looks in his corner already.

Well, deduct a few points for arrogance.

"Vanessa, let's be honest here. I know why you were bidding on that manuscript."

And a few more for impropriety.

He had no idea what the real story was and she had half a mind to tell him where to go. She even drew herself up, bolstering her mental strength while the cutting words formed on her tongue.

Yet as he silently stood there, waiting for her response with a look of—was that *sympathy?*—on his face, she chickened out at the last minute.

"Mr. Harrington—"

"Chase."

"Chase," she repeated, trying to ignore the intimacy of his name on her lips. "I'm sorry, but I don't know you. I don't discuss my personal life with complete strangers—even if that stranger probably hired someone to dig into my background."

He blinked, scrutinizing her in a most disturbing way before he said, "I think I will have that coffee, thanks."

"I'm sorry?"

"You did offer coffee, right?"

"Yes, but—"

"I can help if you show me where—"

"No! No," she repeated more calmly. "How do you take it?"

"Black with one sugar."

She nodded then whirled to the kitchen, her mind one big hot mess. *Coffee. He wants coffee.* She strode over to the cupboard below the sink, opened it to grab the box of Nespresso pods and began to prepare two cups.

The familiar task did nothing to settle her sudden disquiet. Cups from the stand… *What was he up to now?* Spoons from the drawer… *Is he fishing for more information, maybe to go to the press with?* Sugar from the cabinet…

You could try to convince him to sell you the manuscript.

She eyed his broad back through the archway as she warmed the first cup with hot water. Possible. She may not have Juliet's stunning looks and killer negotiation skills but she was still a Partridge. Persuasion ran in her veins.

She dropped the coffee pod into the machine and pressed the button. Yeah, but how much "persuading" would he need?

The brief memory of their first meeting and that weird antic-ipatory...*thing* that had passed between them suddenly flared. The scent of his cologne. The sound of her heartbeat thudding in her head. The moment when she realized how close they were, the exact second his eyes had dropped to her lips...and lingered.

She sucked in a breath, held it for an eternity then exhaled with a snort. Her entire relationship with Dylan had been a secret, sordid affair designed to bolster his fragile ego. And prior to that, she'd been popular because of who her parents were. For once, it'd be nice if a man wanted her just for *her*.

So Chase Harrington thought he knew why she wanted that manuscript? He had no clue. He had no idea how Dylan's re-jection of her—of his *children*—had cut so deeply that it had only now just started to heal. No idea that she'd chosen this new life rather than spend a moment longer in her parents' poi-sonous silent judgment. No idea how desperately she needed some kind of bond, some tangible proof that Erin and Heather's father had been a living, breathing person to her.

As the aroma of freshly brewed coffee filled the kitchen, she took a second to think—*really* think—about her situation. One—she still wanted that manuscript and all it represented. Two—Chase was a businessman, and businessmen lived to make money, right? If she could make him the right offer—

Yeah, but with whose money?

She dropped sugar into his cup then started on hers. By the time she'd finished and returned to the living room, Chase had made himself comfortable.

He'd removed his coat, and it was now draped over the back of the couch. He sat, ankle crossed over knee, looking perfectly relaxed amongst the girls' toys and her comfortable possessions, and her first thought was: he'd make a great portrait subject. Her second: that internet search had done nothing to appease her intense curiosity.

Hedge funder extraordinaire Chase Harrington was worth billions, which was not exactly a selling point given the current financial climate. Yet he was no high-profile Donald Trump: he didn't spend money on expensive cars or private jets. And except for that one standout purchase of a beleaguered midtown office complex, no multibillion-dollar property deals either. For all his connections and wealth, her rudimentary search had come up with less than thirty accurate hits, and only after the usual ones featuring his recent purchase from Waverly's. From those she quickly worked out that, while he owned a few properties around the world, he didn't date supermodels, didn't court the limelight and was intensely private.

Which meant a possibly interesting backstory in there somewhere.

"Tell me, what exactly do hedge fund managers do?"

He took the cup she proffered, palming it in one large hand.

"Well, in simplified terms, they manage a private pool of capital from investors and advise them on trading strategies."

"And what do you get out of it?"

"I put in a percentage, so when the investors make money, I do, too. Plus, there's the investment and management fees."

"So it's like playing the stock market?"

"Sort of." He blew on the coffee before taking an experimental sip. "The term hedging means reducing risk, so it's all about getting as much money as you can for as little risk as possible, then getting out. All funds aren't the same, and returns, volatility and risk all vary. You can hedge anything, from stocks and bonds, to currency, to downturns in the market."

"Like what happened in the financial crisis."

She noted the way his shoulders stiffened, his brow creasing. "Yeah. But that…that was the result of a bunch of arrogant, irresponsible people who—" he took a breath and gave a tight smile "—who aren't really fit to mention in polite conversation. And the only money I manage now is my own and a few select investors'."

She shook her head. "I'm okay at math, but you must have some kind of superbrain to do what you do."

He took another sip of coffee then said slowly, "It's called an eidetic ability."

Her eyes widened. "You have a photographic memory? You're kidding me."

"Oh, I'm not. I was the most frequently requested party trick at college when word got out." His sardonic tone told her it wasn't something he was particularly proud of, which was odd.

A college guy who didn't want to impress everyone, be the life of the party and brag about himself? Intriguing.

"Your parents must be happy you've done so well," she said now.

He made a noncommittal sound and shrugged, which was neither confirmation nor denial. There *was* a major story in his past, Vanessa surmised. One that probably didn't end well, given his response.

So whose does?

In the awkward silence Vanessa sipped on her too-hot coffee, burning her tongue in the process.

"So how did you and Dunbar meet?" he finally asked.

Okay, moment over. "I think we established I'm not going to answer your personal questions."

"I'm not about to go running to the press."

"That's not the impression I got in New York."

He leaned back on the couch, those worry lines marring his forehead again, a sure sign he was uncomfortable. Uncomfortable with being rude? Or because she'd called him on it?

He sighed and suddenly his expression changed. "Vanessa." His cup went down on the coffee table as he fixed her with his direct gaze. "I apologize for my behavior in New York. I was impolite and pushy and totally got the wrong end of the story. I'm sorry." Oh. Those sincere blue eyes held hers and, after a few seconds, his singular attention started to make her giddy, the not-unpleasant feeling a little like a champagne buzz. "I must've come across as…"

She finally found her tongue. "Rude?"

He nodded, stunning her further. "Yeah. I tend to get steamed when people are trying to rip me off."

"But I wasn't."

"I know. Look, this isn't coming out right at all. I made an assumption about you and it turns out I was wrong. Normally I'm smarter than that."

If that didn't beat all. She sat there, unable to form a comeback. Truth be told, he was not at all what she'd first assumed, and she didn't know what to think.

"What would it take for you to sell me that manuscript?" she blurted out.

He shook his head. "Nothing."

"You sure? Just about everything has a price."

Was it her imagination, or did his expression turn bitter? "Not this thing. And anyway, I seem to recall you don't have the money."

"Not everything has to be about money." At the look on Chase's face, she added quickly, "Oh, wow, that came out *so* wrong. I didn't mean… Did you think I…? *Ewww*."

You weren't thinking ewww two days ago, though, were you?

Obviously, he was disgusted by that thought too, because his expression tightened and he rose abruptly. "I've got to be going."

She nodded, her face warm. "I'll see you out."

Vanessa honed in on his broad back as she followed down the stairs, gazing at the efficient haircut closely cropped at the nape. The skin was smooth and tanned beneath his collar— a jogger's tan?

Great. Now she had an image of him running in a clingy, damp T-shirt, his pumped-up arms and legs gliding him effortlessly through Central Park.

Then he was at the last step and she was back in the real world.

Should she shake his hand? Thank him for coming? No, that wouldn't be right. *Say something,* she urged herself as he reached the bottom then slowly turned back to her standing on the last step.

She was nearly eye to eye with him. A disconcerting thought.

"What are you doing Saturday night?"

She wrinkled her brow. "What's on Saturday night?"

"The Library of Congress is having a thing and I'm on the guest list."

"A thing?"

"A formal event. To celebrate some Egyptian display."

"The Tombs of the Missing Pharaohs exhibit?" She crossed her arms, pulling her shirtsleeves over her hands as the cold began to seep in.

"That's the one."

"Aren't you leaving your RSVP a bit late?"

"I'm a donor—I get a bit of leeway."

"Right."

After a moment's silence, he said, "I'm asking you to be my plus one, Vanessa."

She blinked. She had *not* seen that one coming.

"But…"

"But what?"

"Well…" She felt warmth heat her neck again. "I said 'ewww.'"

One commanding eyebrow went up. "I've had much worse, believe me."

"And honestly, I didn't mean it like that."

"Okay."

"Really. I mean, you're an attractive guy. A *very* attractive guy and I'm…" She trailed off, swallowing thickly as Chase's lips quirked. *Okay. I should stop now.*

"So," he said, thankfully glossing over her uncharacteristic loss of control. "Saturday? Just think of it as an extended apology. There'll be food, champagne, culture, adult conversation." His mouth curved again, giving her a tempting sample of devastating charm. "Have I sold you yet?"

"I..." She glanced back down up the stairs, her mind spinning at the sudden turn of events. Her immediate response was to say no. She *should* say no. Her world and Chase's were miles apart. She'd been a part of that world—albeit not at Chase's high end—and had turned her back on it. But deep inside, a gentle insistent tug had started and just wouldn't ease up.

"I'd have to get a sitter," she warned, finally stepping down and walking over to the front door.

"Of course."

She added, "Why are you asking *me?*"

"Why not?" He tempered that statement with a smile.

She swallowed. "What if I say no?"

He slid his hands into his coat pockets. "Do you want to say no?"

Maybe that manuscript wasn't completely lost to her after all. And if one party invitation was all it took to definitively find out, then she'd consider it a good deal.

"Okay. Saturday night."

"Great." He reached past her for the door handle and suddenly her personal space became way too cramped. She took a step back just for the room and air to breathe easier.

Yet his perfectly handsome face, now flush with male satisfaction, made her heart pound against her ribs.

"Thanks for the coffee."

"You're welcome," she replied, picking at a loose thread on her sleeve just so she'd stop staring at him.

I blame you, Mrs. Knopf. Her ninth-grade art teacher had encouraged a healthy appreciation of a well-put-together face, of shadow, form and color and it had stuck, even though Vanessa had long since made peace with her basic art skills.

"I'll pick you up at seven-thirty."

"Oh." She blinked. "I thought I could just meet you there."

"You're not out of my way."

I doubt it was on the tip of her tongue, but she swallowed it back. It *would* save on gas. She shrugged. "Okay." Then she glanced past his shoulder. "Is it raining?"

Chase turned, his profile in stark relief against the porch light and the dark night. "It is." He turned up his collar, dug his hands in his pockets and gave her a small smile. "Sleep well, Vanessa."

She nodded, ostensibly crossing her arms to ward off the chill. But her goosebumping skin had more to do with the way Chase's mouth had formed that little farewell—soft, almost intimate—followed by a small grin that had her wishing for more.

Four

The next few days passed with Vanessa occupied with her job and its familiar dramas—runny noses, sticky hands, finger painting and Bob the Builder. At night she fed, washed and cuddled Erin and Heather, steadfastly refusing to read more into Saturday night than what it was: a way to apologize for his bad behavior.

"A *date?*" Stella, Bright Stars's office manager and Vanessa's friend, had excitedly exclaimed when Vanessa finally owned up to it. "Who with? Not Juan?"

Their UPS guy? "No!" Vanessa had laughingly replied.

"One of the fathers, then. Alec Stein." Stella clicked a button on the computer and the printer whirred into action.

"He's happily married with three kids!"

"Tony Brassel?"

Vanessa shook her head. "Old enough to be my father."

"Not for *some* of us," Stella huffed, crossing her arms across her generous bosom. "John Bucholtz?"

"No. Look, it's not anyone we know, all right? He's from New York."

"Is he rich?"

Oh, yeah. "I didn't ask to see his bank balance, Stell."

"Huh." Stella turned back to the printer and bundled up the papers in the tray. Her tight black spiral curls bounced around her face, emphasizing her smooth caffe latte complexion. "Make sure you wear something nice."

Something nice.

Hours later, after she'd put the girls to bed, she stood in front of her open wardrobe and sighed at the meager selection. Jeans, jeans, pants, jacket, shirt, shirt, shirt…

Reluctantly, her gaze made its way to the back, where a dozen sealed clothing bags hung on sturdy wooden hangers.

Dresses from another world. A world she'd decided never to set foot in again. A world that no longer held any attraction or relevance, not when she had babies to look after and her days were filled with a real job that involved real people. People who entrusted *their* babies to her.

She reached out, drew a finger across one hanger. It had been awkward, stepping back into the role of rich socialite in New York. Like putting on an ill-fitting outfit, something that wasn't designed for her height, weight or coloring, then walking down Fifth Avenue and feeling millions of eyes staring at her. Did she really want to do it again?

But…

Her finger settled on the zipper and toyed with it. She'd be lying if she didn't admit that sometimes she missed wearing a pretty dress and high heels. There wasn't much opportunity for dressing up these days. She hadn't had anything resembling a date since before the girls were born.

Her mouth thinned. Even before then: Dylan was not a man who'd enjoyed going out in public.

She gently shook her head, scattering those thoughts. It wasn't a date: Saturday night was her opportunity to convince Chase to sell that manuscript to her. An opportunity to use all the charm and social skills her parents had paid for. Her purpose as the daughter of Allen and Marissa Partridge had been to sway would-be clients to her parents' practice, charm their colleagues, various political cronies, D.A.s and judges alike.

What was one more?

Ignoring a small tug of uneasiness, she pulled down the zipper with a determined swipe then yanked the cover off.

The Valentino gown sparkled under the light, the bodice of the striking tangerine halter-neck dress shot with silver thread immediately drawing the eye. She turned, pressed it up against her chest and stared at her reflection in the wardrobe door.

Orange generally clashed with red hair, but this particular shade didn't. If anything, it picked up on her titian highlights and brought out the porcelain paleness of her skin. Her mother's skin and hair.

She turned one way, then another. Right. Silver shoes, hoop earrings. A diamanté clutch.

She ran her eyes critically over the long pleated skirt, across the asymmetrical hem. When she finally met her gaze in the mirror, she was surprised to see a smile reflected back.

"It probably won't fit," she said aloud then paused to frown. A few seconds passed, then, "Well, let's just see, shall we?"

The doorbell on Saturday night caught Vanessa on the tail end of her makeup ritual.

"Hmm…early. A sure sign he's eager to see you, sugar," Stella said as she bounced Erin in her ample arms.

Vanessa stuck her head out of the bathroom to glare at her friend. "It's ten minutes, Stell."

"Still, it's interesting." She cooed at Heather who was on her mother's bed, making her way over to the long strand of pearls Vanessa had left on the edge. In one quick movement, Stella scooped them up and put them on the dresser, replacing the necklace with a Winnie-the-Pooh rattle.

"Goo!" Heather grabbed the rattle and gave it a healthy shake. Vanessa grinned.

"Can you go and let him in? I've got this one here."

While Stella went to the door with Erin, Vanessa scooped up

Heather, breathing in her newly washed baby scent all wrapped up in a pink onesie.

With one last look in the bathroom mirror to analyze her makeup and hair, she gave a final nod and walked out.

"Mr. Chase Harrington awaits you in the parlor, Lady Partridge," Stella announced from the bedroom door. As she took a step inside, her face creased into a comical display, lips forming a silent, theatrical, "Oh my God!"

Vanessa huffed back a laugh. "Calm yourself down," she whispered, before giving her friend a gentle nudge as she walked out.

He was back in the living room again, same stance, same commanding presence. But this time she glimpsed a flash of blue silk tie and black suit beneath that luxurious coat.

"Vanessa." Her name rolled off his tongue like something naughty, sending a flush rushing up to her cheeks.

"Chase," she replied, shifting Heather onto her hip as she replied to his smile with one of her own. *Oh my God, indeed, Stell.* He was a stunning specimen. Hard to believe he'd had no date for tonight.

"And who's this?" He stepped forward and it took all of Vanessa's composure not to reel back.

"Heather. Meet Chase Harrington."

"Pleased to meet you, Miss Partridge." He smiled and held out his hand and Heather silently studied it, then him, for a few moments.

That's right, honey, you keep your eye on him.

Finally her chubby face broke out in a smile and she thrust out the rattle.

"Why, thank you." As Chase accepted the offering with a grin, Vanessa felt her breath catch. The genuine smile, the unthreatening distance and the way he bent down to her level… this guy was not only familiar with kids, he actually *liked* them.

To say it threw her was an understatement.

"You look beautiful." Startled, she met his gaze and realized he was talking to her. "Don't you think your mama looks beautiful, Heather?"

"Boo!" Heather replied obligingly then held out her hand for the rattle.

Chase promptly returned it with a chuckle. "Ready to go?"

"Sure." Vanessa glanced back down the hall, to Stella, who had witnessed the entire exchange with a goofy grin.

"Erin's in bed already," Stella said as Vanessa handed Heather over with a kiss.

"I'll just be a moment," Vanessa said over her shoulder before walking swiftly into the girls' room.

"Mmm-mmm, that man is deeelicious!" Stella huffed under her breath, her brown eyes sparkling as she laid the baby down in her crib. "You see the way he was with Heather?"

Vanessa made an affirmative "hmm" as she stroked Erin's cheek, then leaned in to kiss her. "Make sure you put on the night-light. And Heather's still fussy about her pacifier."

"I know the drill, missy. You just go and have yourself a good time."

"It's not a date, Stell."

When she straightened, Stella was studying her, hands on her wide hips. "You're both dressed up, yeah? He's picking you up and you're going someplace with food and alcohol? Sugar, that is a date." She tipped her head for emphasis.

"It's not—"

"Date."

"We're not—"

"Date."

Vanessa gave up. "Okay. Date." She pulled the blanket up over Erin then reluctantly made her way to the door.

Stella's brows went up. "They're fine with Auntie Stella at work, they'll be fine tonight. Now, go."

And with a not-so-gentle pat on the rump, Vanessa was dismissed.

With a deep breath, Vanessa emerged from the bedroom and grabbed her coat from the hook near the front door.

"Ready?" she said to Chase a little too brightly.

He nodded and held out his arm. When she took it, she swallowed the sudden urge to yank her hand straight back.

It was like touching iron draped in cashmere. Delicious and forbidden, something she wasn't entirely sure she could handle. Or needed.

Yet there was nothing to indicate he'd felt it too, not when he smiled at her, nor when he led her out her front door and down the stairs with Stella calling, "Have fun, children!" from the top.

Not even when he chivalrously opened the passenger door on his shiny silver Audi for her.

Chase finally broke the silence a few minutes into the drive. "Nervous about tonight?"

"No," she answered way too quickly. His sharp glance had her adding, "It's only my second night out since the girls were born."

"Really?"

"Well, there was New York. And I don't count last year's Christmas party because I was home by seven."

"So you haven't been out for…"

"Eighteen months." He slanted another look at her, one she couldn't quite read. "What?"

"Hard to believe."

"Not really. I have two babies and that tends to put off a lot of guys."

"A lot of guys are idiots."

She nodded slowly. "Some are."

Then they lapsed into silence for the remainder of the trip.

As they drove down Pennsylvania Avenue, the gentle flutter in Vanessa's stomach had morphed into a serious case of butterflies.

There was no guarantee she'd actually see any familiar faces. And even if she did, it wasn't as if she was scared or anything. But her father had demanded her presence in his world and she'd done that for years, so her sudden disappearance must have raised some eyebrows.

I wonder what they told people.

She glanced over at Chase, his shadowy profile completely focused on the road.

Honestly, what's the worst that could happen? She'd put on her game face and be Vanessa the Socialite, Chase's polished arm decoration for a few hours. *Maybe* she'd bump into an acquaintance or two and have to charm her way around the questions. Either way, she'd been doing this since she was eleven, so it wasn't as if it was difficult.

Second nature. Easy as pie.

And she'd also have time to work her charm on Chase Harrington, although exactly *how* she'd get him to change his mind was a bit of a mystery at the moment. Despite her lack of planning, she wasn't about to give up on that manuscript just yet.

She rolled her neck gently, feeling the familiar pull of shoulder and back muscles stretch and pop into position as Chase drove into the parking garage.

Game on.

She was a vision of aristocratic beauty and poise, Chase thought as they mounted the steps to the impressively lit Jefferson building. She'd done her hair into some kind of Elizabeth Tayloresque updo, the sleek style and halter neck emphasizing her bare shoulders. Her smooth, pale skin glowed, a welcome change from the endless array of tanned bodies. Her only jewelry was a pair of simple silver hoop earrings, and the understatement made her dress—a swirly orange confection—an eye-catcher.

They were nearly at the top of the second flight when her gaze met his and she gave him a small smile.

A smile that somehow made his blood beat a little faster.

And then, something happened. As they took the final stairs and light, warmth and sound hit, her entire demeanor changed.

It was like a curtain coming down: one instant she'd been

smiling at him, the next, every single muscle had tightened, pulled taut into a facade of sickeningly familiar aloofness. When he blinked it had spread to her whole body, from her straightened shoulders to her tilted chin and firm posture.

The Perfect look. The superior, I-am-so-much-better-than-you sheen that made him stiffen in involuntary disgust.

He'd had a moment of uncharacteristic conscience-wrestling during the drive over, debating whether to confess he'd deliberately asked her out knowing a bunch of people from her former life would be here. But then he'd shrugged it off. She'd said yes, right? She was a smart girl: the thought must've occurred to her too.

The truth was, he wanted to see how far he could go to shake her up, throw her out of her comfort zone. Would she crumble under the persona of Vanessa the Perfect or would she handle it with aplomb? Maybe she'd give something away, let something slip that would provide another piece to the puzzle.

As they walked in silence toward the security checkpoint, she kept her head high and her face blank, and every doubt he'd had dissipated. If she could turn the act on and off with apparent ease, what else was she hiding?

With that thought he tore his gaze away from her elegant profile to admire another breathtaking sight—the Great Hall. He traced every familiar line, every step and curve and intricate design of the high mosaic ceiling, the detailed frescoes and sweeping marbled staircases.

The comforting smell of books, of knowledge and history, never failed to center him.

At the designated cloakroom, a haughty blonde took their coats with an insincere smile, but it didn't seem to faze Vanessa. She took their ticket with a cool smile of her own, her back straight and chin so high it gave the impression she was looking down her nose at the entire world.

It was disturbing, watching her go through those motions, when he'd had a glimpse of the other Vanessa already. Or had *that* been an act for him and this flawlessly groomed woman beside him was, in fact, the real deal?

Whatever the answer, tonight would be it. She'd no doubt try to convince him to sell her that manuscript, turn on the charm, most likely flirt. He'd use that advantage to flirt back, assuage his curiosity, prove his point that Perfects couldn't be trusted, then walk away.

Simple.

Five

The soiree had been set up on the second floor in the north-west gallery, otherwise known as the Tomb of the Missing Pharaohs exhibition. It was a fitting backdrop for a bunch of wealthy, fancy-dressed and jewel-laden donors, Vanessa thought. The intricately designed domed ceilings sparkled with subdued mood lights, emphasizing the stunning glass cabinets and displays throughout the room: Egyptian artifacts and ancient scrolls, mysterious mummies and their sarcophagi, centuries-old pottery, canopic jars and surprisingly elegant jewelry.

As they slowly worked the room, Chase introduced her and she made small talk. And to Vanessa's relief, she found she could easily slip back into her old persona, smiling in all the right places and holding up her end of the conversation, on topics ranging from Givenchy's latest collection to the current congressional debate.

Half an hour passed, thirty minutes during which Chase was either drawn into conversation, introduced to someone important or spirited away with a "you just have to meet—" Vanessa let him go then spent another twenty minutes mixing and artfully deflecting blunt inquiries from the few people she recognized. And every time she looked around, she caught Chase watching her. No, not watching…*studying* her with a mixture of bafflement and curiosity was more accurate.

Now, with Chase holding court to a handful of men in the center of the room, she reintroduced herself to Diane Gooding, the library's curator, whom she'd once met on a Winchester field trip.

"Your necklace is interesting," Vanessa said with a smile, nodding at the roughly hammered golden disc ringed with Egyptian symbols. "Did you have it custom made?"

The fiftysomething blonde let out a tinkling laugh, completely at odds with her formal burgundy pantsuit and equally sharp blond bob. "The original is part of Iput's collection. The wife of Userkare, the second pharaoh of the sixth dynasty," she added, nodding toward a glass cabinet on their left. "Nearly four and a half thousand years old." She glanced over at Chase, then back to Vanessa. "I saw you come in with Chase Harrington, correct?"

"Yes."

Diane tapped her chin in thought. "You know, I was beginning to think he was just an alias for another donor. He's never attended one of our fundraisers before."

"Really." Vanessa's curiosity piqued.

Diane nodded to the waiter and lifted two champagne glasses from the tray, handing one to Vanessa. "Yes, he usually just writes a check, sends his apologies and that's it. Until now, of course."

They both turned to study the object of their attention, deep in conversation.

There was a distinct air of power and command surrounding him, and that, coupled with the aura of sexual availability that clung like expensive cologne, made him extremely attractive to the opposite sex. Vanessa noticed the attention he received from the women here. It was like a Pavlovian response, the way those well-groomed heads turned—and lingered—when he entered their line of vision.

And to her consternation, she found herself irritated by it.

Diane sighed. "Beautiful man. Richer than Croesus, of course, and probably owns a good chunk of New York, but intensely private. Some of the rumors are quite outrageous."

"Like?" Vanessa took a sip of champagne, murmuring in pleasure when the expensive bubbles hit the back of her throat.

"Oh, he was married to a sheikh's daughter. He's the love child of some famous actress, politician or oil magnate. Oh, and the best one—a family member is a famous mass murderer." She glanced at Vanessa who'd just snorted in her drink. "See? Crazy rumors."

Vanessa dabbed her lip and refocused on Chase, who was nodding seriously to the man holding him in conversation.

"Whatever his story, you won't see him hosting his own reality show or buying a casino," Diane added.

"No. He prefers keeping his achievements out of the press."

It was a guess, but from what she'd read and heard, a pretty accurate one.

Diane nodded. "A man who gets things done without all that public backslapping. We have a lot of donors like that, especially when it comes to charity. I heard he's a heavy contributor to kids' causes."

Vanessa nodded, even though she had no clue. But it wasn't a far stretch: in the few hours she'd known him, he'd not only mentioned kids and offered up a sleeping technique, but he'd also thoroughly charmed Heather.

So why was he not married with his own kids already?

With a murmured excuse, she left the older woman and made her way over to Chase, a tall, tempting figure in a sea of suits and designer dresses.

"It's all about having ideas, making them known and being able to substantiate them at any moment," he was saying to the handful of nodding men. Their wives, however, seemed more intent on eyeing Chase's broad shoulders, judging by their intent gazes and hushed whispers. "That will get you hired and move you forward in your career."

"Speaking of having ideas…" one woman murmured, and the others chuckled in sisterly solidarity.

"Excuse me, ladies," Vanessa said with a thin smile, gently making her way through the crowd to hand Chase a glass.

He smiled and made a space beside him, earning her a few frowns and a death stare.

Nothing she wasn't used to.

"My son's applied to every hedge fund that recruited at Harvard his first year, but only got two interviews," a man was saying to the rest of the group. "It's a tough field to get into."

Everyone nodded.

"I had very little experience in finance or investment management before I started at Rushford Investments," Chase said.

"So what's your advice then, Chase?"

He took a swig of champagne, considering the question. "Hedge funds love athletes. But they also want to see well-roundedness—the education isn't enough. You have to have the passion, too.

"If he can prove he can do research, that'll put him ahead of the pack. But he'll need to work under a portfolio manager, remember. And the decision to invest will be theirs."

"But he makes money when his investors do, right?"

"Right."

After a few more moments, the crowd dispersed and moved on. Vanessa watched Chase as he slowly shook his head. "What?"

"Nothing."

"You don't think his son can cut it?"

"Maybe, maybe not. It's just—" He took a swallow of champagne, and Vanessa watched his smooth throat work. "Sometimes it's not just about money."

"Isn't that the whole point of a hedge fund? To make money for its investors?"

Chase eyed her, his expression unreadable, before he gave a shrug. "Yeah, you're right."

"Oh, no," she began, stepping into his path as he attempted to recirculate. "I'm not going to let that slide. What were you thinking just now?"

His mouth tweaked, and before she knew it, a smile slowly spread. "Vanessa Partridge, are you asking me a personal question?"

Her body tensed, the trace of heat and intimacy coming from him disturbingly distracting. "Is it personal?"

He shrugged again. "Some people get into this career to make money, and check their ethics at the door."

"But you didn't."

"I have a very clear line when it comes to legal and moral obligations."

"'With great power comes great responsibility.'"

One brow went up. "A Roosevelt quote."

"Actually it was also in *Spider-Man 2*."

He snorted in amusement before adding, "Harry Potter too, I believe."

She couldn't help but grin back.

"So…are you having fun?" he said.

Her smile dropped a little. "What do you think?"

"I think," he said slowly, watching her brush a curl of hair behind her ear, "that you're trying very hard to pretend that your back and neck muscles don't ache. That you're tired of people asking you the same questions. And that you'd much rather be at home, with your girls." At her silence he tilted his head. "Am I right?"

She stared at him for a long moment then finally nodded.

"So why did you actually agree to come out with me?" he asked.

"Because I wanted to wear a nice dress and heels?"

He shook his head. "Nah." When he placed his palm flat on the wall behind her head, his arm an inch away from her face, her eyes widened.

When he leaned in, she tried to suppress a faint gasp and damn, was that *satisfaction* she detected behind those blue eyes? He was actually *happy* about the way he affected her.

When his lips hovered close to her ear she had to force her body not to react.

"If this is you trying to persuade me to sell you Dunbar's manuscript, it's going to take more than just one date."

She jerked back, glaring at those way-too-close charming blue eyes glinting in amusement. "Two dates, then?" she said tartly.

His deep chuckle doused her anger, replacing it with arousal as his warm breath fanned over her cheek. She bit her lip to stop a groan escaping. When had he so thoroughly demolished her personal space? Worse, now she actually felt *nervous*.

Nervous? She'd trained that useless emotion out of her system years ago. Yet here he was, making her sweat, and worry and... *Breathe*.

If she stood very still, maybe he wouldn't... Oh, no. She felt his mouth brush the top of her ear and suppressed a shudder as he murmured, "You are something, Vanessa Partridge. A Perfect. But you're definitely not the type to offer yourself up, *Indecent Proposal*–style, am I correct?"

"You..." She had to close her eyes to gather her composure as her heartbeat quickened. "You don't know that."

"Hmm." He eased back to study her, his eyes unreadable. "So what are you offering?"

Her eyebrows went up. "What do you want?"

His tight smile did nothing to calm her nerves. "I want many things, Vanessa, but I suspect you're slightly out of my league."

She gave a soft snort of disbelief. "You're kidding, right? You're Chase Harrington, hedge fund billionaire and I'm just—"

"Money and position are irrelevant. It's all about what you're born into, what you grow up with. Tell me, Vanessa Partridge..." He leaned in again, giving her a chance to back away, but she refused to let on that he intimidated her. "Are you actually offering to warm my bed in exchange for that manuscript? Or have I got that wrong?"

She felt desire jerk her to life, sparking something deep down in her belly where it sat buzzing, heating her from the inside out. His eyes, his sudden quickening breath told her he was interested, but his cool, almost contemptuous eyes screamed the opposite.

Lord, what was she getting herself into?

"Because," he continued softly, his head dropping and his mouth way too close to her ear again, "that would be very tempting." He shifted, and now she could feel the heat coming off him in waves, despite the distance. It did nothing to quell the surge of need swelling up inside her, even though he'd yet to actually touch her.

"Nessie!"

He suddenly pulled back, cool air rushing in to fill the void, and Vanessa took a bolstering breath as her body cried out at the loss.

They both turned to watch a tall, lean, impeccably dressed guy with dark floppy hair approach them, a broad smile showing off perfectly white teeth. His eyes were latched so firmly onto Vanessa that Chase felt the sudden urge to snake his arm around her waist and stake his claim.

Which was all shades of ridiculous.

"I haven't seen you in ages, Nessie! How the hell have you been?"

"I've been great," Vanessa replied, turning her head ever so slightly to receive the cheek kiss. When her eyes met Chase's, he could swear he saw them ice over.

"James Bloomberg, Chase Harrington," she said by way of introduction.

As they shook hands, James frowned. "Harrington... Have we met before?"

"No," Chase replied smoothly.

James tapped a finger on his chin. "You look familiar... A

client, then?" At Chase's blank look, he added, "Partridge and Harris? The Washington law firm?"

"No."

"Well—" James turned to Vanessa with a broad grin "—soon to be Partridge, Harris and Bloomberg. Bet you're kicking yourself now, hey, Ness?"

"Indeed." When Vanessa smiled, Chase could practically see the insincerity drip off her lips. He hid a smile of his own.

"Ness and I used to have a thing going, years back." James leaned in and added sotto voce, "It was all hush-hush. Her father never knew. Hey!" He barked to a passing waitress. "Get me a scotch rocks, can you?"

"I see," Chase said. He'd bet his left hand that Allen Partridge had known exactly what was going on with his daughter and this clown.

"So, it's been a long time, Ness. Two years, right?"

"Something like that."

"Your father said you're teaching? University?"

"Toddlers."

"Ouch." He gave a theatrical shudder. "And they pay you for that?"

Chase watched Vanessa's jaw tighten, her green eyes hard. "That's usually the way it works. So, how have you been, James?"

When he dragged his hand through his hair and shot her a charming, lopsided grin, Chase barely managed to hide an eye roll. *Oh, come on! A totally practiced move if ever I saw one.*

"Working," James said. "You know the drill. Heavy client load, no sleep." He took the glass from the waitress without a backward glance or a thanks. Chase caught the woman's thin-lipped glare before she turned away. "The workload is *insane!* But I can't complain."

"I think you just did."

James paused, his glass halfway to his mouth, before he laughed. "I see you haven't lost that old snarky streak, Nessie-girl."

She smiled. "And it's good to see all your ass kissing finally got you somewhere, James."

James threw back his head and laughed again, then swallowed some scotch. "God, I missed that humor! Always good for a laugh, you were. So," he added, running a frankly intimate gaze over her bare shoulders and neck, "fancy going out sometime?"

Dude, I'm standing right here! Chase scowled, resisting the overwhelming urge to voice an immediate refusal. Jeez, what was wrong with him?

With gritted teeth, he slowly swiveled to Vanessa, chomping down on his irrational reaction as he lifted one questioning eyebrow.

She shot him a glance then returned to James.

"Thanks, James, but—"

"Uh-uh." He gave another one of those sickening I'm-so-charming grins and put a hand on his chest. "Don't break my heart by saying no. I don't get much time off as you know, and we have lots to catch up on."

Huh. Chase knew exactly what kind of "catch up" this jackass had in mind. And to his surprise he felt that crazy heat of anger begin to swell. It flared when James the Jerk put a hand on Vanessa's bare arm and gave it a gentle stroke.

His fist involuntarily tightened by his side but instead of going with his instincts and clocking the guy, he said, "Yeah, Vanessa. You haven't seen each other in years. You should catch up."

She shot him a look laced with irritation then shifted her weight, which forced James to drop his hand.

Good.

"Honestly, James, I'm totally shot with work and I—"

"Ahhh." He shrewdly glanced from Chase to Vanessa. "Not stepping on any toes, am I?"

Chase heard Vanessa sigh. "No. But between work and my children, I have no spare time. Sorry."

"You have kids?" Alarm flickered across James's face before he quickly cleared it and took a step back. And man, it just made Chase's desire to punch him even stronger. "Yeah. Well," James said, looking visibly flustered. "I gotta—" he tossed a thumb over his shoulder "—go mingle."

Vanessa nodded. "Sure. It was good to see you again, James."

The guy glanced from Chase, back to her. "Yeah. You too."

"Nice to meet you, Jim...Jimmy...Jimbo," Chase said smoothly and gave him a not-so-gentle manly thump on the shoulder, gaining no small amount of satisfaction in James's sudden frown as he left.

Chase finally turned to her, taking in her tight-lipped countenance. "Why didn't you say yes?"

"You're kidding me, right?" She smiled at a few passing people. "James Bloomberg is an ass and I don't go out with asses."

"You did once."

"Yes, well, I was young. I learned by trial and error. Let's go look at the displays." Even as her mouth stretched to return the greetings from those she knew, there was something missing from her eyes. That, plus he could feel the tight coil in her body with every step.

"Why do you do that?" he finally said as they neared a gently lit alcove displaying a massive hieroglyphic-laden vase.

"Do what?"

"You've had this look ever since we first walked in. The same one you had at Waverly's. It's like—" he searched for the right word "—a mask."

She blinked those perfectly made-up green eyes. "A mask."

"An aura, then," he amended. "Whatever it is, it changes you. Makes you all cool and aloof. Untouchable."

She was silent for a dozen seconds or more, the white noise of conversation a persistent buzz in the background. "My sister calls it my game face," she finally said with a faint smile. "You'd have one, too, if you spent your entire life in my parents' world."

"Fundraisers, political dinners, lots of career opportunities."

"Exactly."

"The curse of being popular, huh?"

Chase had meant to sound light, but it came out way too jagged and hard. So, of course, she frowned.

"Says he who's constantly surrounded by guys hanging off his every word. Hello, pot?" She lifted up her hand, mimicking a phone handset. "It's the kettle here. You're black."

Chase snorted. "It hasn't always been like that."

"Of course not."

"Seriously. It's not my reality."

"So what is?"

"A small crappy town, with crappy people and even crappier kids."

That silenced her for a moment, until he added, "Your sister embraced the life."

Her smile became mocking. "Ah, yes. Juliet Partridge, the glamorous divorce lawyer to Hollywood's stars. The success of the Partridge family. How proud my father was the day she passed the bar exam."

"You didn't want to be a lawyer?"

"My father's dream, not mine. I realized that as soon as I got into Harvard. So I changed my major and he refused to speak to me for a whole year."

Such a casual reply yet so laden with hidden meaning, from the tilt of her chin to the way she didn't meet his eyes. "So you went into teaching. Did he finally forgive you?"

She took a sip from her glass and glanced over at the crowd. "Well, when I graduated he gave me a new BMW and got me a job at Winchester Prep."

"But not—" Her sharp, shocked intake of breath cut him off and he followed the direction of her gaze, to a group of old boys drinking and laughing near the sarcophagus display. "Something wrong?"

Her piercing green eyes grazed him before skipping back to the men. "My father's here."

Ah, right. That. He refocused sharply. "Which one?"

"In the middle. Tall, silver hair, red tie."

As they both watched, a man leaned over and whispered something in Partridge's ear: the next moment he was returning their stare.

Vanessa groaned. "That's done it." She turned her back and took a deep swallow of champagne before stabbing him with accusing eyes. "Did you know he was going to be here?"

Say no. Quick. But he'd hesitated a second too long, long enough for Vanessa's eyes to narrow and her breath to stutter out.

"You son of a—"

"Vanessa."

It was impossible to ignore such a deep, commanding voice, even if the man wasn't her father. Chase studied Vanessa as she swallowed again, gave him a furious glare then turned. But in that nanosecond, just before she turned, she did that thing again, the same donning of the mask when they'd first arrived.

For her father.

"Dad." She smiled, all tight lips and controlled emotion as she leaned in, placing a polite kiss on his cheek. "I didn't know you were here."

"Of course you wouldn't." Partridge turned his steely gaze to Chase and offered his hand. "Allen Partridge."

"Chase Harrington."

They shook. Strong, firm grip, Chase noticed. Classic domination tactic.

"Harrington," Partridge repeated, finally releasing him. "Not related to the Boston Harringtons?"

"No."

Partridge's eyebrows dipped, still thinking. "So how do you know my daughter?"

"Dad!" Vanessa interjected. "That's none of your business."

Chase smiled thinly. "Don't you really want to ask what I'm doing with her?"

"Chase!" Now Vanessa looked mortified, a flush spreading over her cheeks.

Partridge crossed his arms. "Yes."

"I asked her out tonight—she said yes."

"You do know she has two babies?"

"That's it!" Vanessa hissed, shooting a fire-laden glare at her father. "You have no right butting into my life like this!"

Partridge appeared unruffled. "You're the one who's back in my 'shallow, insensitive, controlling' world now, Vanessa. And full disclosure is always better at the start of a relationship."

"Again, none of your business."

"And anyway, I know," Chase interrupted. When Vanessa's eyes snapped to him, he deliberately put a possessive arm around her waist. "There's not much I don't know about Vanessa."

Her eyes widened as her mouth dropped open to form an adorable little O. He could feel the rising tension in her body, even as her mouth tightened and she stood her ground. With the devil riding him, he left his arm there, binding her close.

Chase nodded to the now-silent Partridge giving them the speculative once-over. "So you're a library donor too?"

"Corporate Gold Tier," he said. "You?"

"Same."

"Not a lawyer, are you?" Partridge smiled, yet his eyes remained humorless.

"Financial analyst."

"Which company?"

"I'm an independent."

"Right."

Oh, he was good, implying everything and nothing in that one little word, and for one second Chase questioned the wisdom of provoking the man. Unscripted questions meant unpredictability, and while Chase normally thrived on a certain amount of unpredictability during a normal business day, Allen Partridge, on the other hand, made an excellent living out of it.

For the second time that night, discomfort shot through him.

Vanessa remained silent, scrutinizing their exchange with a wary eye. "Chase runs a hedge fund."

"Right." Same word, completely different meaning. This time, a small judgmental frown creased his brow. "So how were the last few years of the financial crisis for you?"

"I didn't bet on the crash or throw people out of their homes, if that's what you mean."

"Good to know," Partridge returned, although his entire manner suggested otherwise. "Where did you say you were from again?"

"New York."

"I see."

And no doubt he'd be checking up on those details by the time the evening was over. Not, Chase thought, that he'd find anything incriminating. He'd flown under the radar for years. Still, the thought of this man rifling through his past rankled.

"Juliet's at the house," Partridge was saying to an oddly silent Vanessa. "She just finalized a huge settlement between that movie producer and his second wife."

"Instead of getting them to reconcile? That's a change. You must be thrilled."

Partridge frowned, flicked a glance at Chase, then back to his daughter. "I don't think I like your tone, Vanessa."

"What tone?"

"You know the one." As Partridge continued to frown, Chase could practically see the inner debate raging: Should he push it with Chase there? Or wait until another time?

Much to Chase's disappointment, he chose the latter.

"William's been asking about you," Partridge went on, his gaze scanning the crowd.

"Has he?"

"Yes. He still has some of your things. You should give him a call."

She nodded. "I might." She paused, frowning as Chase downed the rest of his drink. "What's that look for?"

"What look?" Partridge said.

"Oh, come on, Dad. It's me you're talking to here."

He darted a glance back at Chase. "I was wondering if Chase was the father."

Chase's sharp, shocked breath was drowned out as Vanessa choked on her champagne and ended up in a coughing fit.

He thumped her on the back once, twice, before she shook her head and stepped out of his reach. "You're kidding me, right?" she finally got out.

Allen shrugged, unperturbed. "I thought—"

"See, Dad, that's where you go wrong every single time," she gritted out. "You don't have to think about these things because it's my life and if I chose to screw it up, I'm totally okay with that. Chase?" Vanessa whipped her head in his direction. "Let's go."

"Right." He gave Partridge a polite smile. "Excuse us, will you?"

And without further comment, he drew Vanessa away. They made it through the crowd, to the other end of the room, before halting at a massive cabinet that displayed the glorious artifacts of an entire dynasty of Egyptian royals.

She dragged in a few deep breaths then placed both hands wide on the cabinet, staring down into the display with furious intensity. Her smooth brow wrinkled, long fingers curled around the cabinet corners, back tense and rigid.

Man, was she steamed.

"Who's William?" He murmured to her profile.

"The Principal at Winchester Prep," she muttered then glanced up at him. "So, did you get what you wanted, setting me up like that?"

Chase stuck his hands in his trouser pockets with a shake of his head. Apart from the last fifteen minutes, she'd been *too* perfect tonight, her interactions and conversation too artfully delivered. She'd obviously done this many, many times before; not surprising, considering who her parents were and how she'd been brought up.

It was an act, one she'd been born to play year after year.

Yet seeing her with those people out there, then her father and that James guy, only emphasized the fact Vanessa Partridge had left that social circle for a reason. So why did she hate that life so much? And why had she turned her back on it? There was obviously some friction with her father, but you didn't just toss all that money away because of a family argument.

What's happened in your life, Vanessa?

As a boy he'd pulled apart his fair share of clocks and radios just to see how they worked. His mother had shut that down real quick when she'd found him at the kitchen table, her precious Mixmaster in pieces. His attraction to complex systems had eventually led him to finance, and to this day, he still needed to know how and why things worked.

Vanessa was one of those conundrums.

"I needed to see—" he began.

"What?" she scowled. "See what? How I'd react to the life I left behind? How much I'd squirm from all the questions? How I'd handle seeing my father again?" She shoved her hands on her hips, her face contorted into sharp, angry lines. "Why would you be such a jerk?"

Yeah, why? "I…"

"It was a test, wasn't it? So, how'd I do?"

"Vanessa…" He winced.

"No, tell me."

"You were…perfect."

"Right. You can take me home now." She whirled and headed off toward the arching entrance, her heels on the marble floor echoing in the cavernous interior.

Chase moved swiftly to keep up then halted her with a hand on her arm.

The contact drew a harsh intake of breath from her.

"You also had an ulterior motive for this evening," he said.

She stared at him, her wide eyes almost luminescent under the soft light. "Let…" She swallowed and his gaze went right to her throat, then back up to her rounded eyes. "Let me go."

Vanessa clamped her mouth shut. Dammit. That had

sounded more like a plea than a demand and she hated that. Worse, her righteous anger was slowly leeching away under his cool reasoning.

He finally released her. "This wasn't a real date for either of us."

Oh, way to make a girl feel special there. She scowled. "I know."

"Not when we both have too many questions. When you want what I have and I have…well—" his gaze swept her face, passing all too briefly over her lips before returning to her eyes "—not nearly enough answers."

This, she realized as his dark gaze captured hers. *This is why you really said yes.* Her heart leaped, jumping around in her chest in crazy anticipation. Like a smitten teenager she mocked, pressing her lips nervously together, the smooth slide of lipstick a welcome distraction. Until his gaze transferred to her mouth and it felt as if everything stopped altogether.

She scowled. "If you'd only just…"

"Just what? Asked you what I want to know? After you'd finished telling me to mind my own business?"

"Bringing me here to see my father isn't the way to go about it."

"I didn't exactly know he'd be here."

"Really." She glared at him, wishing she could drag the truth directly from his brain. But boy, the man had *such* a poker face. "And by the way, you don't want to piss off Allen Partridge."

"Huh. Well, he doesn't want to piss me off, either." Chase crossed his arms.

"He has a lot of power and influence on the East Coast."

"So do I."

"Really. Because from what I've heard tonight, throwing your weight around isn't your thing."

"What have you heard?" His expression turned guarded.

"I know you're not flashy with your money and you don't abuse your influence. I know you donate to a bunch of charities, mostly for kids. And I know you couldn't get away from your childhood quick enough."

A scowl flashed across his brow, displeasure darkening his eyes.

"I majored in early-childhood psychology. 'To know the man, first know the boy,'" she added.

With an exasperated snort he said, "Freud?"

"No." She shrugged. "I read an interview with Hugh Laurie once and it just stuck. Doesn't make it untrue."

He paused then shook his head. "You are—" he let out a sigh, his breath brushing her skin "—an intriguing woman, Vanessa Partridge."

"Not really."

"Yes, you are."

As anger slowly leeched away, Vanessa could feel every tiny inch that separated their bodies, every lick of warmth from his broad-shouldered presence that curled into hers. Her bare skin tingled as though he was emitting some weird kind of phero-mone, one that made her muscles go all trembly and nervous.

Worse, she could feel her game face slipping.

"We…we should go."

To her surprise, he nodded. "Yes."

It felt like an eternity before he broke eye contact, but when he did she breathed in a relieved sigh, one that faltered when he put a hand gently on her elbow and led her down the long corridor.

Stop touching me. She closed her eyes briefly before amend-ing it to, *No, scrap that thought. Keep doing that.* Because it'd been ages since a man had showed her this much attention. Chase was a great-looking guy. And they'd already shared a few moments, moments in which she'd managed to see under the hard shell to the man beneath.

There were lots of beautiful women here tonight and he'd had every opportunity to return their flirtatious looks, but she'd witnessed nothing but polite decorum on his part. Yet for her, he'd been attentive, touching her not once but a dozen times, his hand a casual yet telling brand on her back, her arm, her elbow. She'd secretly enjoyed that, even though it made her jump every time.

Then there was his million-dollar smile, one that made her insides go all fluttery. And the moments she'd caught him unawares, staring at her with a look that Stella would only describe as "hungry eyes."

Oh, he was interested. And yet, he didn't trust her.

Her insides lurched. Was Chase the kind of guy who didn't particularly care who he bedded, as long as they were willing? That couldn't be right.

Unfortunately, it could turn out to be all too real. In which case, she was better off walking away now.

Six

As they approached the closed cloakroom door, his hand left her arm, leaving a faint warm impression. Vanessa sighed. "It's closed."

Chase tried the handle. It gave way. "Not for long. Come on."

"But what about—"

"The Ice Queen guarding the coats?" He swung the door wider and the shadows inside seeped out around them. "She won't be back until later. Still—" he glanced over his shoulder "—we should hurry just in case."

"But—"

"Have you always been a rule follower, Vanessa?"

Her mouth tightened. "No."

"So let's go." He jerked his head toward the racks.

It was all the encouragement she needed. She stepped over the threshold and Chase closed the door behind them.

For one moment absolute blackness engulfed them, until a bright light appeared and Chase's iPhone illuminated his features.

"Got the ticket?"

She held it up then stared at the racks. "I can't figure out the system."

"Let me." He took the slip from her, his fingers brushing hers for one brief second, sending a dangerous flame over her skin.

Just as she'd done before, she forced it away. Only this time, it was getting harder to keep everything at bay.

You can't. You shouldn't.

But damn, she wanted to. As he focused on finding their coats, Vanessa focused on wrestling with her subconscious. She'd heard a lot about Chase Harrington these last few hours, who he supposedly was, all his outstanding achievements, all the money he made. The room had been abuzz with his sudden appearance and she'd deftly redirected the more probing questions when people had realized they'd arrived together.

She didn't particularly care that someone, somewhere, would most likely get mileage out of that bit of gossip: what concerned her more was Chase. Something about him still jarred. It was as if there was something vital missing, some important piece of information that, when revealed, would make complete and utter sense.

Like explaining this sudden attraction to a guy who was the poster child for everything she'd left behind? Right.

She stared at Chase's back, nibbling on her thumbnail before quickly dropping her hand. No, James was that guy. Had been *her* guy for a few brief, stupid weeks when she was eighteen.

"Do you know I've been compared to my older, smarter and infinitely prettier sister for close to twenty-seven years?" she finally said. Chase paused, glancing at her over his shoulder. "Twenty-seven years of being expected to act, look and think a certain way—the Partridge way. Which meant law school, perfect grades, and after graduation, an internship at my parents' law firm. In ten years, possibly less, I'd be offered a partnership—if I brought in the right clients and worked fifteen hours a day, seven days a week."

She had his full attention now.

"Some people would kill for that opportunity," he said.

"Yes, they would. But…" She sighed. "I wanted something different. I wanted to teach, have a family of my own. Have a life and not just a career. And *my* life, not something my father had mapped out since I was a toddler."

He paused, then asked, "And was Dunbar a part of that something different?"

"I'd thought so, once." She turned her head away from his intent gaze. "Dylan wasn't a risk taker. He even triple-checked his seat belt." She snorted. "Ironic really, considering he died in a plane crash in the middle of nowhere."

"Indonesia, wasn't it?"

She nodded. "Unsafe plane, bad track record. I really don't understand why he was there. It wasn't like him at all. Too many indefinables."

"Maybe he was doing research or branching out to explore other cultures." He rubbed his neck. "Getting in touch with his spiritual self."

"Right." She raised one eyebrow. "He knew *exactly* who he was."

"You don't think much of him as a person, do you?"

She frowned. "I didn't say that."

"But you meant it."

She gave a quick apologetic glance heavenward before refocusing on him. "When I told him I was pregnant he walked out."

"So he left you with two babies and no financial support."

"You make them sound like unwanted pets! He didn't *leave* me with them."

"But he *didn't want anything to do with you. Or his children.*"

Oh, how brutal the truth sounded coming out like that. Vanessa didn't know what to say. She'd been the biggest risk of all, and one Dylan ultimately couldn't cope with.

"He always said he never wanted kids." She shrugged, halfheartedly flicking through a row of hanging coats. "I didn't believe him. I mean, would you believe it from a man who wrote books like that? A former English teacher, who was also an exceptionally talented writer? A writer who pretty much defined a generation and enthralled the entire world?" She shook her head. "How can someone *not* love kids when they write like him? People loved him. Everyone flocked to his signings and appearances like he was some kind of modern-day pied piper. I saw it time and again, over and over."

But from a distance, remember? Never at his side, never part of his entourage. Miranda, his brittle blonde publicist who spent every minute with one eye on the clock. Max, his jovial editor who consistently overlooked his unmet deadlines because Dunbar was their number-one cash cow. And even Aaron, his snarky assistant who pulsated an irritating "I'm better than you" aura. But not her.

And she'd been naive enough to be one of those "I can change him" women.

"Talent and douchebaggery are not mutually exclusive," Chase said. Then added, "Just take a look at your James."

"James Bloomberg?" She frowned. "He's not *mine*."

"Once upon a time he reckoned he was."

She sighed and returned to the coats. "I was eighteen. We went out twice and he spent the whole time talking about himself. And," she added, her eyes narrowing, "we went *dutch*."

Chase couldn't help himself. She looked so indignant, her whole body all tight and offended, that the laugh just came out.

"Chase! It's not funny!"

"Of course it isn't." He bit back another chuckle. "Sorry." He reached past her and grabbed a coat—her coat—off the hanger then held it out. After another glare, she slowly slipped her arms into the sleeves.

"He was only trying to get to my father through me," she added, turning to face him as she dragged the lapels together. "Just one of the many fakes and users I've had to deal with my entire life."

"Until you left."

She looked up at him, her eyes shadowed in the darkness. "Yes. When I told my parents I was pregnant, they went ballistic." Her features twisted, her mouth flattening. "And when I refused to tell them who the father was, we had a huge screaming fight."

"Why didn't you tell them?"

Her snort echoed in the small room. "You don't know Allen Partridge. To my father things are either black or white, no shades of gray. He *adores* the law. So when something is wrong, it's wrong. He would've sued Dunbar for child support regardless of my feelings in the matter. Can you imagine the frenzy that would've caused?"

Yeah, he could.

She nodded. "I wanted normality for my girls, not notoriety as the illegitimate children of D. B. Dunbar. And my father said some pretty unforgivable things, too. So I left. Everything."

She really had left everything, Chase realized. She'd not only turned her back on her parents' Victorian-style mansion in affluent Washington, the Partridge status and all that entailed, but also her family. The entire life she'd known. Everything familiar and comforting and easy.

She'd left her life, just like he had.

"You weren't tempted to demand a share of Dunbar's estate?"

"No." She turned back to him, her face partially hidden by shadows. "If he'd wanted me to have something, it would have been in his will, right?"

He shrugged. "Still, it must've been challenging, especially since you were pregnant."

"It was. It *is,* every day. But it was the best decision I've ever made."

When he nodded, she added, "Is that what you did? Leave everything behind?"

He paused, feeling the full weight of her interest behind her casual question.

Tempting…but no. He could practically smell the curiosity rolling off her, yet beneath those waves he also sensed a genuine interest.

Yeah. Just because she'd asked didn't mean he would tell her. Distrust was a familiar companion, one that had served him well over the years.

He turned to grab his coat from the hanger. "Like you, it wasn't working. So I made a conscious decision to change."

He felt her eyes on him as he applied himself to the task of straightening his collar.

"From a small town boy to a billionaire hedge funder," she said softly. "That's quite a change."

"I work damn hard for it." He finally glanced up, her impassive expression at odds with her eyes, dark and full of something he couldn't quite make out.

"And from what I've heard tonight, you give away a lot too."

He shrugged again, a response that was beginning to bug Vanessa. Was it because he was so clearly low-key when any other guy with his track record would've called a press conference and taken out an ad in the *New York Times?* It was odd, seeing someone like Chase actively pursue normality while her parents thrived on the opposite, publicly declaring each and every achievement to the news-hungry world.

It was also very clear that she'd get no more answers until she gave a few herself.

"I met Dunbar at my parents' firm," she said softly. He watched her, his expression neutral as they made their way to the door. "I'd been doing some research for one of the entertainment lawyers and recognized him. You've got your coat wrong," she added, nodding at his collar.

He reached up and fiddled with it as she continued, her hand on the doorknob.

"He ended up going elsewhere but was flattered I knew who he was. He asked me over to his place and me, being the starstruck fan I was, said yes. I ended up in his bed. It lasted six months. No, you've still got it… Here, let me." She reached up, smoothing down his suit collar before refolding his coat over the top.

Satisfied, she glanced up at him with a smile…only to have it freeze at the look reflected in those dark depths.

Careful, Ness. You're treading a very thin line here. She quickly took a step back and swallowed.

"Why did you really want that manuscript?" he asked softly.

"For Erin and Heather," she replied without hesitation. "Dylan left them with nothing, not even an acknowledgment he was their father. I have nothing tangible to remember him by—no notes, no gifts. There's not even a photo to show the girls later, when they start to ask questions.

"I wanted them to have this one thing, something personal and private they could connect with when they were older. Dylan always made copious notes on his drafts and sometimes it revealed more than he wanted the world to see, so he always shredded them. And hopefully it would've given them an insight into who he was, maybe understand his drive and passion a bit better." *And understand why he chose to leave?* She paused, swallowing the last bitter words before they managed to taint the air. It wouldn't do to still be angry, she reasoned. It wasn't healthy. "So, Chase," she said. "What's your real reason?"

She could tell he was spinning the words around in his head, working out what to tell her. And this made her sad somehow, even though they didn't really know each other and he had absolutely no reason to trust her.

Which meant he was debating whether to tell her something important.

They remained still for a good few seconds, studying each other in the shadowy light.

"You've heard of the Make-A-Wish Foundation?" he finally said.

"The charity that grants wishes for terminally ill children?"

"That's the one."

She paused then offered, "That's an expensive wish."

"It's something I wanted to do, not an official one." As she opened her mouth, he cut in with, "That's it, okay?"

"But—"

"There is no 'but.'"

"But if it's not official then the wish must be for someone you know."

"Vanessa," he warned, his voice deepening. "You need to drop it."

"*Is* it someone you know? Is it—"

With a soft curse, he was in her face, all broad and scowling, and she felt a sudden frisson of danger spark. Just like before, only a thousand times more dangerous because weren't they now alone, in the dark, with the knowledge of the evening heavy between them?

"That's it." Her eyes rounded. "I knew it was personal!"

He was practically breathing down on her now, his mouth an angry slash. "Jesus, Vanessa, why can't you just be satisfied with that answer and be done with it?"

"Oh, no." She shook her head. "You did *not* just say that to m—"

With a frustrated growl his mouth slammed down on hers, cutting off her words, then her thoughts, then her breath.

Lips that looked so soft were now so very hard. They ground into hers, bruising, punishing, while his hand gripped the back of her head, firmly holding her in place.

Righteous indignation flooded in, urging her to react, but in a millisecond it evaporated. Chase filled her senses—his scent, his heat, his lips. And as his mouth continued to slant across hers, forcing a response, blood pulsed under her skin, sending a familiar anticipatory quiver to the most intimate parts of her.

So she shocked them both by molding her body to his and kissing him back.

She opened her mouth and allowed him access, his murmur of surprise lost in the tangle of their tongues. Yet she couldn't help but groan when he pulled her closer and the full heat—and hard, intimate weight—of him pressed insistently into her belly.

Oh, wow.

She grabbed his face in her hands and tore her mouth from his. "Chase."

His eyes were dark and dilated, his breath heavy on her lips. "Yeah?"

"We're in a cloakroom."

"I know."

The warmth between their melded bodies flared, igniting a desperate yearning deep inside. She wanted to weep in frustration but instead she took an unsteady step backward. "A *public* cloakroom. Anyone could walk in."

She waited for him to catch up. A heartbeat later, his mouth flattened and one hand went into his hair. "Right. Wouldn't want that."

There you go.

So why did the disappointment feel like bitter ashes on her tongue?

She took a deep breath, but it wasn't enough to hold the charged air. "Chase... I think..."

"We should go."

She nodded, unable to form the words because right now, her throat felt rough and scratchy from a bunch of inexplicable tears. Which was stupid. She wasn't the weepy, emotional type at all.

So she straightened her shoulders, swallowed thickly and put on her game face.

"Are you ready?"

At his nod, she turned, grabbed the door handle and yanked it open.

Light speared in, followed by the faint sounds of the reception still going strong. Vanessa blinked away the spots of light as she strode out, looking for all the world as if she hadn't just kissed Chase Harrington in a darkened cloakroom. And didn't want to keep on kissing him.

That walk to the front entrance was interminably long, the wait for Chase's car even longer. She occupied herself with keeping warm, her hands in her pockets, her breath a foggy huff on the air. She'd been warm only moments ago, when Chase had been pressed up against her, his mouth on hers.

Dammit, why was she wishing they were back in that cloakroom?

Finally they got into the car and were on their way home. And still not a word between them.

He hadn't apologized, but then, she hadn't really expected him to. Chase Harrington just didn't seem the type to regret kissing a woman.

He probably kissed a lot of them. Hundreds. Thousands.

She scowled into the night as the lights sped by. *Oh, you cannot actually be jealous?*

With a small shake of her head, she sighed. *So what have we learned this evening, apart from Chase Harrington being a fabulous kisser?*

That he'd had a crappy childhood. That he was intensely private. And that he'd spent a million dollars on a child's dying wish. Someone that meant something to him.

That little puzzle piece latched onto her heart with all five fingers and squeezed.

"When are you leaving Washington?" she finally ventured in the cavernous silence.

He shot her a curious look. "Monday morning. Why?"

"You should come over for dinner tomorrow night. If you're not doing anything, that is," she added.

Another look, this time emphasized by a frown. "After everything that's happened tonight, you're inviting me to dinner?"

She shrugged, grateful he had the road to focus on. "I get the feeling you don't get a proper home-cooked meal often."

"Mostly takeout or restaurants."

"Well, I can't guarantee restaurant quality—" she smiled tentatively "—but I've been told my roast lamb is pretty good. If you don't mind eating at six and with messy twins."

When they stopped at a set of lights he gave her his full

attention and for a moment, Vanessa felt the enticing pull of those clear blue depths. *Imagine going up against that when you're negotiating a million-dollar deal.*

He wore "charismatic and charming" as effortlessly as that expensive suit, using it to great effect when he needed to, but other times totally unaware of how devastating just one smile could be.

Well, unaware most times. If you didn't count that moment back at the library. And in the cloakroom.

Oh, great. She swallowed. *I know what you're thinking and you should stop it.*

It wouldn't work. He lived in New York. He was incredibly rich. She was a working single mom who'd turned her back on the limelight and corruption that money could bring. And what guy would jump at the chance of dinner with a couple of unpredictable babies anyway?

There you go, Ness, overthinking things again. He never said he wanted a relationship, and frankly, you don't have the time for one either.

But that didn't mean she couldn't just enjoy herself.

She sucked in a breath. Oh, yes, he had the kind of face and body she'd definitely enjoy. He was so...so...*male.* That was it, he was a man in every sense of the word, so broad and rugged that sex practically oozed from him. So unlike the quiet, bookish intelligence of Dylan, plagued with self-doubt and in constant need of ego-stroking and affirmation.

Chase Harrington would be a perfect rebound guy. No strings, no commitment. That is, if he was actually into it too. He might not be. That kiss may have just been a one-off and he wasn't—

"What?" Chase asked suddenly, shooting her a quick glance, and she realized she'd been staring at him as her thoughts ran crazy in her head.

Just brilliant.

"It'll just be a meal," she reassured him—or herself—feeling her skin flush as the lights went green and they set off.

"If I've learned anything in life, Vanessa, it's that things are never as simple as what people would like to think."

She crossed her arms. "Fine, then. Don't."

"I didn't say I didn't want to."

She sighed. "So what *do* you want, Chase?"

He glanced at her, but his expression was tough to interpret in the dark.

"I would like to have dinner with you tomorrow night. Thank you."

"Good." She nodded, and a funny, almost delighted anticipation filled her chest.

Seven

On Sunday, through a batch of laundry, then vacuuming, Vanessa couldn't stop thinking about Chase. Even bundling Erin and Heather up for a quick grocery run wasn't enough to completely occupy her.

That kiss had been so dominant, so very me-Tarzan, that it surprised her even now. What did that say about her, letting him go all caveman on her? That she'd actually liked it?

She was being naive and unrealistic. Chase was married to his job, which meant any woman would have to be content in second place. And then there was that whole "distrustful" thing he had going on.

Yet he'd bought the manuscript for a sick child.

Even though that contradiction warranted more scrutiny, she put it out of her mind, put the girls down for their naps then took up a large sheet of white paper and began to fold.

She stayed engrossed in the origami for another hour, until Erin and Heather woke, and she began to prepare lunch. After an hour of play, they went down again and Vanessa was inevitably left alone with her thoughts and a silent apartment.

Thinking about last night made her skin burn. Thinking about seeing him again tonight had her insides doing all sorts of exciting things.

Well, no wonder, she rationalized, abandoning the tiny, complete swan for dinner preparations. She hadn't been on a date in ages, much less kissed a guy. And Chase was a highly intelligent, incredibly successful guy.

Eventually, the afternoon light lengthened, her apartment began to fill with the delicious aroma of roast lamb and her attention returned to her origami.

Two hours later, the doorbell rang.

With a fussy Erin on her hip and Heather in the playpen, she went down the stairs. When she opened the door, Chase filled the empty space.

This time he was in jeans, a white unbuttoned shirt and blue sweater, his long coat over the top. A casual Chase but just as mouthwatering as the night before. More so because he looked as if he could be any other working-class guy in her neighborhood instead of *someone who commanded billions on a daily basis.*

Yet he wasn't just any other guy, especially after last night.

Her mind suddenly roared with the memory of their kiss, the way his lips had felt, his breath on her skin. And, more tellingly, the reason she'd stopped him.

People could walk in.

She was fully aware there was a zero chance of walk-ins in the privacy of her home.

Then a grumbling Erin shattered the moment and she came back to reality with a thump.

He held up a bottle. "I brought wine but wasn't sure if you drank it."

"Now and again," she managed to reply through her tangled thoughts. "Come on in."

He nodded at the irritable baby in her arms. "Is this Erin or Heather?"

"Erin." She gave him a wry look as she mounted the stairs. "She's normally the quiet one."

After his chuckle petered out, every single step up to her apartment sounded inordinately loud, the echoing clunk an odd accompaniment to her giddy anticipation. Her mind spun. Anticipation of what—another kiss?

No. Definitely not the impression she wanted to convey to her children.

Chase closed the door behind him then shrugged out of his coat, hanging it on a spare peg. "Something smells good."

"Lamb roast," she said over her shoulder as she went to Heather, who was cheerfully bashing a rattle on the playpen bars. "With veggies and bread. Hope that's okay?"

Chase rested his hands on the plastic edge of the pen and peered in at Heather. "Sounds perfect. You want me to watch Erin?"

She blinked, taken aback, but quickly covered it. "Oh, okay."

"I grew up around kids—I've held a baby before." The small quirk of his lips had Vanessa's face warming.

"Here you go, then."

She handed Erin over, who proceeded to just stare at him.

"Ma! Din!" Heather demanded from the pen.

"Dinner is soon, sweetie," Vanessa confirmed, gently bending down to cupping the little girl's head with a smile. "I'm doing it now, okay?"

"'kay."

"You good in there?"

"Good."

Chase grinned as he followed Vanessa into the kitchen, Erin a silent bundle in his arms. Man, babies were warm! She practically seethed heat, her brown curls hugging her head, an identical match to her sister. Yet unlike Heather, all smiley and content in her playpen, Erin's huge brown eyes just stared at him as he tried a tentative grin.

When he breathed in deep, filling his lungs with that familiar baby smell, his heart tightened at the memories. Mitch and his crazy, happy family, how they'd welcomed Chase into their lives without judgment or criticism. For months he'd been deathly afraid of rejection, of Mitch's widowed mother getting sick of him and finally sending him packing, so he'd consciously made an effort to pull his weight—washing up, cleaning, taking care of the little ones. And after a year, he'd finally relaxed enough, even though the fear still gnawed in the back of his mind.

They'd never rejected him. It was Chase who'd done the rejecting, years later.

He stroked Erin's soft head as the memories swirled, marveling at the soft curls beneath his palm.

Erin simply stared back at him.

She had her mother's intense look. She'd also inherited that silent, slightly superior stare, he realized, his mouth stretching. And she was damn cute, too.

"Bet you'll have all the boys wrapped around your finger," he said softly. She simply shoved a fist in her mouth, glancing around for her mother.

"Huh. Guess you haven't made her good list yet." Vanessa smiled as she picked up a bread knife and began splitting the rolls.

"Playing hard to get. I like a challenge."

Vanessa retrieved a plate from the cupboard and transferred the rolls onto it. "Be thankful she's not screaming her head off."

"Oh, I am."

Vanessa laughed and when their eyes met, Chase grinned back.

Dunbar was an absolute idiot.

He'd read up on the guy before the auction, but newspaper articles, websites and blog mentions provided a skewed perspective depending on whether they loved or hated the man's work. Knowing what he'd done to Vanessa though, that…that was the kicker.

What kind of person walked out on his pregnant girlfriend, ignored his own kids?

"If you scowl at her like that, she's liable to start crying."

"What?"

She glanced up from the carrots she was chopping. "Must be something nasty to produce such a frown."

"Yeah."

Vanessa let the silence pass for a heartbeat, then forged on with, "Tell me something."

"Mmm?" He went back to smiling at Erin, but she refused to be drawn into his charm. Sensible girl.

"Why is it you're not married?"

His expression froze then he dragged his eyes to her.

"I mean, you're thirty-two, rich, good-looking," she said with barely a trace of awkwardness. "Incredibly tolerant of babies…"

"I'm not interested in marriage."

"Any particular reason why?"

"It's unnecessary, not to mention a financial minefield." He shrugged. "Why complicate things in a perfectly good relationship?"

"Wow," she breathed. "You sound exactly like my sister. Except—" she returned to cutting up carrots with single-minded focus "—if it weren't for marriage, she'd be out of a job."

"Exactly. I just don't see the point. You don't need a piece of paper to make you happy. And one out of every two marriages fails, so…"

"Wow, that's a cheery thought."

"It's true. Marriage changes people. I've seen it over and over."

"And was your parents' marriage like that?"

"They were *exactly* like that."

At Vanessa's look, he swallowed the rest of that incriminating sentence. "There's no point in being with someone if it doesn't make you happy," he said, then added, "Did Dunbar make you happy?"

She paused, thinking. "I think it was more a case of total hero worship. I mean, he could be oh so charismatic and witty—a real charmer with the ladies. But he was also a stickler for privacy. When he wasn't promoting his books, he'd refuse publicity shots and interviews. He wasn't one for going out either."

"That must've been restrictive for you." He slowly put a wiggly Erin down and kept an eye on her as she toddled over to a chair.

"Yes, it was." Her gaze lingered on Erin then came back to him. "But I also had my job to consider, too."

"How?"

"We're talking about Winchester Preparatory College here. An elite private school. We had the kids of politicians, lawyers, movies stars and bankers. The faculty signed nondisclosure contracts with exclusivity and morals clauses. Rich Washingtonians are deadly serious about their children's education and the morals of those teaching them."

"What, the school was against any of their staff forming relationships?"

"No. But me being pregnant and unmarried would have been grounds for an inquiry. A reprimand at the least, at worst, termination. And after the strings my father pulled to get me there…well…you get the picture." When he nodded, she opened another cabinet. "Wine?"

"Sure."

Vanessa uncorked the bottle then poured a glass for him, half a glass for herself.

When she handed him his drink, his fingers connected with hers for one second, sending a shot of warmth to his gut.

"You seem to be doing pretty well there." She nodded to Erin, who had finished with the chair and was now attached to Chase's leg.

"Just call me the baby whisperer."

She grinned. "Did you have younger brothers and sisters?"

"Only child." He snorted. "My mother couldn't have coped with more."

"But you've had practice with small children."

He hesitated. "My best friend—Mitch—had two younger sisters and three brothers. I spent more time at their house than mine."

"That's a lot of kids." She picked up two plates with an assortment of vegetables on each. "Do you see them much anymore?"

"No." He nodded to the high chairs at the end of the table. "Do you want me to strap Erin in?"

"Please. I'll get Heather."

One more little piece of the puzzle so grudgingly given, Vanessa thought as she walked into the living room. How on earth did he ever get close to anyone, make a connection, when he was so suspicious of everyone's intentions?

The answer was obvious—he didn't.

And that made her a little sad.

"Come on, baby," she cooed at Heather, then scooped her up from the playpen.

"Do you need me to do anything?" Chase asked from the doorway.

"If you could set the table that'd be good."

"Done."

As he laid out the plates and cutlery, Vanessa removed the steaming lamb from the oven. Over her shoulder, she could hear him talking with the girls and she smiled.

Chase Harrington was turning out to be one big, honking surprise after another.

As usual, dinner turned out to be totally Erin-and-Heather-focused: a messy, vocal affair that seemed to hold Chase's attention for the duration, she noticed. He watched her feed the girls in part bemusement, part analytical scrutiny, and Vanessa was aware of his gaze the entire time.

The topic of dinner conversation started on neutral ground—work—when Vanessa wasn't making eyes at Erin and Heather, making exaggerated faces and gently encouraging them to eat. But as they began to relax and Chase let down his guard a minuscule inch, she got a glimpse of the real person behind the polished exterior. A guy with a fantastic knowledge of movies and composers, an amazing aptitude for figures and facts and a deep, burning drive to succeed. A guy who automatically wiped a splash of apple from Heather's cheek with a smile. A guy with whom the girls seemed perfectly content.

A guy who, despite the evening's conversation, was still very much a mystery.

She slid him a glance as Heather took her final spoonful of pureed apple. Whatever he was assessing, she hoped she passed. She sensed that, once his mind was made up, Chase would stick by that verdict.

She also suddenly realized that she cared what he thought of her. She really shouldn't—he was just one man, and a gazillionaire at that, a guy she probably wouldn't have met under normal circumstances. But he'd somehow wormed his way under her skin, tugging at her compassion, making her smile, making her care.

And let's not forget he makes you hot and bothered.

Yes, she'd quickly found herself intrigued by the light and shadow that was Chase Harrington.

"So what made you choose finance as a career?" Vanessa asked as she wiped Erin's high chair down.

Chase was stacking the dishwasher and she ran her eyes appreciatively over those wide shoulders and back, then down to the trim waist.

Very nice…

"Money." He closed the door and turned and she barely managed to refocus her gaze someplace G-rated. "I wanted to make lots of money."

A loud burp split the air and they both laughed.

"Good girl, Erin!" Vanessa exclaimed then added to Chase, "Your family…they didn't have very much growing up?"

"Oh, they had enough."

At her confusion, Chase said slowly, "My father was a minor local celebrity. He owned the biggest bed store in the county and ran a regular ad on the local TV station."

"Sounds interesting."

"Oh, it was something, all right."

At her confused look, he added wryly, "Let's just say his loud, cheesy ads did not improve my high school experience."

"Oh." Vanessa winced. "Not good, huh?"

"'Let me get you into a bed!'" he boomed out in an exaggerated Texan drawl.

"Excuse me?"

"That was his catch-cry. Mad Max Harrington of Mad Max's Beds. It was...excruciating." He eyed her, his face unreadable as another fragment of the puzzle fell into place. Then he promptly changed the subject. "So, you do origami?"

At her questioning gaze, he nodded toward her living room. "The stack of paper, plus I noticed two new animals on the shelf. A bird and a bear, right?"

"Koala and kookaburra, actually." She smiled. "My parents' last housekeeper taught me. It's my creative outlet after a day of boisterous kids."

"You're very good. Must take a lot of patience."

"And nimble fingers." She wiggled her digits for emphasis as she walked into the living room with Erin and placed her in the playpen. "Needlework and knitting never appealed, my musical skills are just bearable, and I can't write or paint. So origami it is." She began wiping Heather's chair down, then her face.

He had his hands in his pants pockets, leaning against her counter and looking so intimately at home amongst her things that she felt a sudden fierce urge to go up and touch him, to see if his jaw was as hard as it looked, then take a deep breath and fill her lungs with his seductive male scent.

Wow. Where had that come from?

She lifted Heather out, her warm cheek pressed against her baby's hot little body.

Hormones. That's all.

"So what do you do when you're not buying expensive manuscripts?" she said, putting her daughter gently on the floor.

"I work."

"Apart from that."

He gave an amused snort. "That's about it."

"What about winding down?"

He paused, thinking. "I run."

Now she was getting somewhere. "Just for fun or...?"

"I've done a couple of half marathons when work permits." He watched her go through the motions with Heather, grinning when the baby let loose a champion burp. "And I collect a few things—some art, sculptures, a few books."

"Books?" Vanessa eyed the toddling Heather, who was studiously batting at a magnetic toy stuck to the fridge door.

"First editions for the investment. But I read novels for pleasure."

"I would've thought you'd be too busy."

"It's amazing how much time you waste at airports. Plus, I've loved books ever since I learned to read. It's important to make time for things that give you great pleasure."

She scrutinized him for a moment then shook her head with a soft sigh. "You are so not what I expected, Chase Harrington."

"Which was?"

"A bigheaded, arrogant, money-hungry fat cat."

He smiled, his direct gaze holding hers, warming her from the inside out for long seconds. "And you are not what I expected either."

She raised one eyebrow. "Do tell."

"A stuck-up, spoiled, better-than-you princess." His grin took the sting out, but only just. Is that how he'd seen her?

"But I *do* have a trust fund," she reminded him.

"And a BMW from your father."

"Ooh, now you're ruining it." She winced, then bent to pick up Heather.

"Sorry."

"Apology accepted." She walked toward the playpen and leaned in to scoop up Erin. "Time for a wash and change."

When she thought now would be a perfect time for Chase to make his excuses and leave, he surprised her by simply nodding. "I'll make coffee. How do you take it?"

"You don't have to stay, you know."

His eyebrows went up. "Is that your way of asking me to leave?"

"No, I… Wow, that did sound terribly rude, didn't it? I just meant this is probably a little boring for you, so if you want to go…"

"Vanessa, I assure you, I am not bored. Now, coffee?"

She blinked, giving him a small smile. "Milk, no sugar."

He nodded. "Okay, then."

She bathed the girls in record time, dressed them in their pajamas then walked into the living room as the wonderful smell of coffee permeated the air.

He nodded to the cups on the coffee table. "All done." His gaze automatically went to Erin as she swayed unsteadily towards the furniture. "Good thing you have corner protectors on that coffee table. It looks just the right height to do some damage."

Vanessa nodded. "Yep. Heather, right here." She pointed to the middle of her forehead. "Once was enough."

He took a seat while Vanessa scooped up a grumbling Heather.

"Okay, baby." She sighed. "The playpen it is."

She placed Heather in the pen and smiled as the girl promptly picked up a shape cube, sat and started to gnaw on it.

"She would spend every waking moment in there if I let her," she said with a shake of her head as she reached for her coffee. "She loves it."

"It's probably a security thing."

She looked up at him curiously. "What do you mean?"

"Four walls, enclosed space. It's a defined, finite area, so she's comfortable in it."

When she remained silent, studying him, Chase felt like

kicking himself. *Dude—just because your head's full of useless facts doesn't mean you have to share them all.*

Yet he had a feeling about this side of Vanessa, as if he could say practically anything and she'd listen without judgment or negativity. As opposed to the Vanessa of last night, when he'd felt his tongue tie up and his palms sweat just by being in her Perfect presence.

And that kiss...

Oh, man. He thought he'd managed to sufficiently ignore that dumb lapse in judgment, but obviously not. Who could ignore the way her lips had felt, her murmur of pleasure and the promise of what they could do to each other, naked and alone in bed?

He'd kissed women before—lots of women, once he'd gotten over his surprise that they'd wanted *him*. Vanessa was just another Perfect who happened to turn him on.

He had to stop with that. She may have started out as one of them, but she sure as hell wasn't one now.

"You're right," Vanessa said suddenly.

He blinked. "Sorry?"

"The playpen. It's like when babies are born—after forty weeks of a tight, enclosed space, they're delivered into a huge, empty void. They need to be wrapped for the first few weeks to get used to the space."

Chase nodded, his gaze leaving Heather to watch Erin edge her way around the couch, gripping the sturdy support with tiny hands. When she finally got to him, she clung firmly to his leg, her huge brown eyes staring straight up into his face.

"Up!"

He grinned. "Well, since you ask so nicely..."

She grinned back, raising her arms, and he obliged.

As Erin settled herself on his lap, the room fell into silence and for the first time in a long time, Chase wasn't on the receiving end of pointless chatter just to fill it.

Silence was nice. More than nice. It was...something he couldn't quite define. Comfortable, maybe? Yeah, comfortable.

He took in Vanessa, now lying stomach down on the floor and sticking her fingers through the playpen to tickle Heather's toes, making them both giggle.

Maybe not "comfortable." Vanessa's neckline dipped, revealing the curves of her breasts and he quickly glanced away before slowly returning.

The view was way too tempting.

Yeah, stop.

Then he glanced down at Erin and his smile widened.

"*Psst*. Vanessa. Look."

She looked over on the tail end of a grin, eyes creased and mouth wide and for a second, Chase felt something shift inside. Something warm and arousing and definitely unexpected.

Then her gaze landed on Erin and her face sort of crumpled.

Erin had clambered up into Chase's lap and fallen asleep.

Oh, my. Vanessa's insides constricted. That had to be the most adorable thing she'd seen—Chase with a goofy, perplexed smile, and Erin in her cute Winnie-the-Pooh onesie, chin tipped up, mouth slightly open and snoring gently.

She stifled a giggle.

"That's hilarious," she finally managed to say, pulling a strand of her hair from Heather's eager fingers.

"Do you want me to put her in her crib?"

"If you don't mind."

He rose fluidly, his large hands cradling her daughter with firm confidence. She watched him walk down the hall, her mind a jumble of mixed emotions, before she scooped Heather up and followed him.

"Thanks," she said. "I'll be out in a moment."

She took the time to completely focus on settling Heather, trying to ignore the scene she'd just witnessed in her living room, firmly refusing to read into it even though her heart had begun to thump in the most annoying way.

She saw fathers with their babies all the time. And every time it made her heart ache with part joy, part what-might-have-been. But with Chase and Erin…gosh, it was as if her insides had melted or something.

A deep, strange yearning rose, sending her thoughts off on crazy tangents before she firmly got them under control. Instead, she refocused on Heather and the Dixie Chicks song she'd been humming under her breath.

Ten minutes later, Heather was asleep and Vanessa padded quietly down the hall. To her surprise, Chase had his coat on.

"You're going?" she blurted, cringing inwardly at how desperate that sounded.

Chase nodded. "I have an early flight tomorrow."

"Okay." There was no way she was going to ask him to stay. So instead, she opened the door and indicated he go first.

The cold air rushed up to greet them as they descended and Vanessa shivered, wrapping her cashmere hoodie tightly around her waist.

Chase unlocked the entrance door then turned to her. "Thank you for dinner. I haven't had a meal like that in a long time."

"You're welcome. Erin and Heather seem to like you."

"They're cute girls. Very—" he searched for a word "—unscreamy."

She laughed. "Oh, they can bring the roof down. Luckily I have forgiving neighbors."

He grinned and Vanessa crossed her arms to combat the intimate warmth that quickly flared. "You'd make a great father, you know."

His smile faltered for one second before he said, "Good night," and leaned in, kissing her softly on the cheek.

Oh. Just a brief warm brush of those lips and it was over. Her disappointment must've shown, because when he pulled back a bare inch, he gave her a curious smile, then inhaled as if he was about to say something but then thought better of it.

"Chase…" His name on her lips came out all wrong, almost like an appeal, but she didn't have time to fix it because in the next moment he bent forward again with a soft groan and *really* kissed her.

Oh, yes, it was as delicious, as exciting as she'd remembered. His mouth slid over her bottom lip, the generous swell of flesh warming, teasing, arousing. Again, her breath escaped in a familiar rush as her heart sped up. Her eyes fluttered closed and she let the moment take her.

The cold air from the open door goosebumping her flesh. His deliciously masculine scent teasing her senses. The ache in her calves where she'd stretched up with way too much eagerness.

They were joined only by their lips, his heavy breath mingling with hers as he slowly deepened the kiss. Her mouth opened willingly, allowing his tongue in to play and tease, sending her heart rocketing and a low throb begin in the pit of her belly.

She wanted this to go on forever, wanted this reckless, out-of-control feeling to carry her away and make her forget everything, just for a while. But even as she breathed him in, and her entire body started to heat up, he gently withdrew.

No…! She squeezed her eyes shut and tried to follow, but it was too late. Cold air rushed in to fill the empty space, grazing her lips and forcing her eyes open.

Dammit.

"Good night, Vanessa," he repeated, but this time the rough timbre behind his farewell was unmistakable, as was the dark look in his eyes.

"Do you want to…" She hesitated, unable to form the words. *Come back upstairs and stay the night.*

She desperately wanted to say it, and if she were living another life, she would have. But she was a mom and her girls depended on her to set rules and boundaries.

As much as she wanted Chase, she would never compromise those principles to have him.

He made a soft sound, something halfway between a groan and a curse. "I have to go. I'll call you."

"Okay."

When he walked out and down the porch steps Vanessa took a bolstering breath, the sharp night rushing into her lungs like a slap of reality. He wouldn't call. Once he was in New York, wrapped up in his real life, there'd be no reason to.

He already had his answers and his manuscript.

With a sinking heart, she watched him walk down the path. But at the end, just inside the pool of light, he looked back at her with a smile that turned her insides to mush.

Maybe it was a good thing he wasn't staying. Because she had this awful feeling she'd never want him to leave. And that was something she instinctively knew he would do, eventually.

Her father's cutting words rang in her ears like harbingers of doom. Men like Chase Harrington wanted perfectly groomed, no-baggage, society-ready women. She'd been that once.

There was no way she could be that again.

Eight

Thirty thousand feet in the air, twenty minutes out of Georgia's Atlanta airport and Chase finally looked away from the stocks report on his iPad to glance out the window.

The air was clear, the early-morning sun blinding. He squinted for a few seconds before pulling down the shade with a sigh.

The strange yearning that had dogged his departure last night hadn't eased up. It confused him.

Chase Harrington hated confusion.

In his briefcase, bound and boxed in special acetate-free paper, lay Dunbar's precious manuscript. Despite his turmoil, a small smile tugged at his lips. Sam was going to be speechless when Chase finally revealed the "special surprise" he'd been hinting at for the last week.

He'd been anticipating these few days with Mitch and Sam since the auction. It was a bittersweet feeling, wanting to see Sam again yet knowing every time he did, he was one step closer to…

His smile dipped to a frown. He had to be strong, had to

suck it up and keep on going. This wasn't about him, it was about Sam and what he wanted. A terminally ill nine-year-old didn't need tears, or worry or fear. He needed strength, needed people to say it was okay. He needed hope, however futile the inevitable outcome.

Chase had that, all bundled up in his briefcase. That was his purpose here, not obsessing about some weird feelings he had when he was around Vanessa Partridge.

He was attracted to her, plain and simple. Nothing weird about that. Totally normal. She *was* an attractive woman, after all.

One whose soft voice had floated gently down the hallway, singing a song he'd instantly recognized. He couldn't get out of there fast enough—until he just had to go and kiss her.

Idiot.

He didn't do commitment. And Vanessa was the poster child for it.

His mind was still churning when he disembarked, collected his bag and drove an hour north to the Mac-D Ranch.

"He's sleeping," Mitch said after he opened the front door and they shared a brief hug. "That's all he seems to do. He's lost interest in his books, TV, the Playstation. You didn't have to buy him that, by the way."

"I wanted to." Chase followed Mitch down the long hall to the guest bedroom. "We never had anything like that when we were Sam's age. Your mom couldn't afford it and I…"

"Yeah," Mitch scowled as he swung the guest bedroom door wide. "Your folks were too wrapped up in all their crap."

Chase slapped a hand on Mitch's shoulder. "I have something that might interest him."

"Like what?"

"Remember when he started talking about D. B. Dunbar's last book?"

Mitch's face tightened. "How he said he wouldn't be around to read it?" He puffed out a breath, his eyes closing briefly in pain before they sprung open. "Damn near broke my heart that day."

"Well, I got it."

"What, the book? But it's not due out until next year."

"No, the actual manuscript."

"You got the…" Mitch frowned then stared at Chase. "How did you manage *that?*"

"Man, you have got to start watching the news." Chase finally dropped his bag on the bed then unzipped his carry-on. "The manuscript came up for auction last week and I bought it."

"You bought it," Mitch repeated slowly, staring at the package Chase pulled from his bag. "Just like that. How much?"

Chase grinned, waving the sheaf of wrapped papers gently in the air. "More than a newspaper, less than a mansion."

Mitch's hand went through his shaggy hair then came to rest at the back of his neck. "Dude, you really don't need to keep buying this stuff. No, listen," he added when Chase tried to interrupt. "It means a lot—no, everything—that you're here. Honestly, I can't tell you how grateful I am that Sam's last six months have been spent out of that hospital, in the comfort of his own home. You bought the specialist equipment, paid for all those tests, a nurse. Olivia's been brilliant, by the way," he added. "Hell, you also brought in Tom to cook—"

Chase put up a hand. "I need to stop you right there, because I know where you're going with this. I want to do this and I can more than afford it. This is me you're talking to, okay, Mitch? We've been best buds since junior high. I'm Sam's godfather. I didn't do anything all those years ago to help you, so please, let me do something now."

Mitch shook his head. "I've told you, there's nothing you could have done."

"I could've returned your calls."

"When you were in the middle of that whole insider-trading mess? No," Mitch said firmly. "I completely understand. Seeing your boss go down in flames…that kind of crap can screw with your entire life for months."

Chase remained silent, his past failure a faint, bitter memory. If anything should be a lesson in misplaced trust, Mason Keating—Rushford Investment's senior manager, his former mentor and now criminal at large—was it.

He sighed now, tossed the package on the bed and loosened his collar. "This is about making Sam happy, not me assuaging misplaced guilt. And I know this will make him happy. You know it."

Mitch cupped the back of his neck and gave his head a shake. "It will."

"See? No problem." Chase smiled. "Now, what say we grab a beer and you can get me up to speed with life in the slow lane?"

Mitch choked out a laugh, the rare sound a welcome relief to Chase's ears. "Slow lane? Ten thousand head of cattle is hardly slow, dude. But don't say I didn't warn you…"

When the phone rang on Monday night, Vanessa tore herself away from the televised Columbus Day parade to answer it.

It was Chase.

She nearly dropped the phone in shock.

But then he called again, same time Tuesday. Then the next night. By Thursday, she was anticipating the phone's soft ring with schoolgirl glee, something she'd never done before.

At first she stayed on noncontentious ground, talking about work, then movies, books and the places they'd visited: Vanessa and her family ski trips to Colorado and Christmases in Hawaii, Chase with his travels across Texas, Arizona, Nevada. But gradually, by Thursday night, their conversations had branched off into various likes and dislikes, childhood experiences, future challenges. Yet Chase still skimmed over some of her innocent questions, which made Vanessa even more determined to find out more.

"Tell me something about you," she began as she settled on her couch with a blanket and a cup of coffee then flicked the TV volume down.

"I had a new piece of art delivered today."

Not what I meant, but still… "Which one?"

"A Gainsborough. It was part of the Cullen collection."

"The collection that Waverly's was auctioning off?"

"Yep. A very small but very expensive portrait."

"You like Gainsborough?"

"Well, it's an investment, so…"

"Do you ever buy anything that's not an investment?"

His deep, frankly intimate chuckle reverberated in her ear like a caress, making her shiver. "Food. Clothes. Travel."

"Okay, so…tell me something else about you."

"Like what?"

"Like…did you live in Texas your whole life?"

She heard the pause, a second too long. "Until college."

"And you didn't keep the accent."

"No, ma'am," he drawled, making her smile. Then, "I worked hard to lose it."

"Why? I think it's charming. Very Matthew McConaughey."

"It was more of a disadvantage than anything."

"I bet the college girls loved it," she teased, taking a sip from her cup as she glanced briefly at the soundless TV screen.

A brief pause, then, "Not really."

"I find that hard to believe."

"Yeah, I wasn't that kind of guy."

"And what kind of guy is that?"

"The jock who partied every weekend, had a dozen girlfriends and got by on charm, off-color jokes and a football scholarship."

Was that a thin veil of disgust she could hear? Vanessa frowned. "That's right, Mr. Photographic Memory." She affected a tone of gentle playfulness. "Gosh, you would've been an awesome study partner. I was always a last-minute crammer. How I got my degree I'll never know."

His huff of laughter meant she'd hit the right note, and Vanessa breathed out an inaudible sigh.

"Says the girl who scored a job at Winchester Prep."

"They had hundreds of applicants, mine included. I'm sure my father's influence gave me an unfair advantage," she asserted. "But let's not talk about him."

"Okay. So how's the weather?"

Vanessa laughed. "Oh, smooth segue, Mr. Harrington."

"One of my many talents."

"Many, huh?"

"Mmm-hmm." That soft, deep hum in her ear sent her skin prickling and she swallowed, steeling herself against the delicious, involuntary sensation.

"Like?"

"I can name the last thirty Oscar winners in the Best Director category."

"Handy for when we play Trivial Pursuit. Anything else?"

"What did you have in mind?" His voice had taken on a deeper timbre, and dangerous anticipation suddenly swirled in the air.

Vanessa closed her eyes, squeezing her thighs together as an unexpected spark of desire flared. She was enjoying their banter way too much. "Like—" Then she glanced at the TV and frowned. "Oh, great."

"What?"

"Waverly's is on the news again." She grabbed the remote and flicked the screen off, the mood broken. "Poor Ann."

A pause, then Chase said slowly, "You and Ann are close."

"Close enough. She and my sister stayed in touch even after Juliet moved. I really like Ann—she's smart, tough, doesn't gossip and is completely loyal to her friends. She's worked very hard to get where she is."

"And made a few enemies, by the looks of things."

"Who hasn't? Waverly's woes sell papers and Ann's love life just makes it more titillating. If the CEO were a man, the press wouldn't be half as brutal."

Chase paused. "You're probably right."

"I know I am. Female execs are judged on their physical appearance and emotional suitability all the time. When a man is tough, he's assertive. When a woman is, she's a bitch. And no one ever asks a man to choose between his career and marriage." She paused to take a breath. "Sorry. I'm ranting, aren't I?"

"Not at all."

She snorted. "Now you're just being polite."

"Vanessa," he said with a smile in his voice, "you should know by now I'm not 'just' anything to be polite."

"I'm...not sure."

"Of what?"

Of everything. Of you. Of this. "You're not an easy read, Chase Harrington."

"I can't afford to be."

"In business? Or in your personal life too?"

Silence.

Vanessa stilled, her hand tight on the phone. Would he actually answer that or dance around the topic again?

Finally, he said, "Both. Vanessa?"

"Yes?"

"I believe you're getting a bit personal."

"Am I?" she said lightly, sliding down into the couch and crossing her ankles over the armrest.

"You know you are. So let me ask you something."

A faint anticipatory throb started up in her chest. "Ooooo-kay..."

"What perfume do you wear?"

She blinked. "Sorry?"

"There's this smell about you, vanilla mixed with something else, something almost powdery that I can't quite figure out. It's driving me nuts."

She was driving him nuts.

Her breath rushed out in one huge whoosh.

The palpable silence throbbed as he waited for her reply, but all she could do was listen to her heart going crazy.

He'd been thinking about her.

She reached up and pulled the elastic from her ponytail

and the newly washed curls fell over her shoulders like a soft kiss. She shivered.

"The vanilla is my hair conditioner," she finally said. "The other is probably diaper-rash cream."

Oh, man! As soon as it was out, she rolled her eyes and mugged at the ceiling. *Way to kill a mood, Ness.*

"Diaper-rash cream," Chase repeated.

"Mmm-hmm." Vanessa squeezed her eyes shut, her lips pressed tight.

"Interesting. Vanessa?"

"Mmm?"

"What are you doing on the weekend?"

She wound a curl around her finger, first one way, then the other. "Oh, the usual—washing, cleaning, cooking, tending to babies. You?"

"Why don't you come to Georgia?"

"What?"

There was yet another pause, long seconds during which Vanessa tried to unravel the tangle. "Chase, Georgia? Why would I—I can't afford—and I have the girls and… What's in Georgia?"

"Me. And my godson, Sam."

The confusion cleared with those few words.

"You're in Georgia?" *Wait, hang on.* "You want me to meet your godson?"

"Yes. He has leukemia. It's terminal and I promised I'd read him the last Charlie Jack book."

A handful of replies swam in her mind, all congealing into an inadequate ball of excuses. Finally, she said, "Sam is your Make-A-Wish child."

"He is. He…"

She waited with a held breath for Chase to continue, until her head practically spun from lack of air. Eventually he said, "I'd like you to read the book with me. If you want to."

Oh. This was big. So very, very big. How long had he

chewed this decision over and over, debating whether or not to include her in his tight, private circle?

It meant progress and that meant scary relationship stuff. Stuff she wasn't sure she'd be any good at, considering her priorities would always lie with her girls, first and foremost.

Erin and Heather, who'd been born perfectly healthy.

She gripped the phone, squeezing her eyes shut. "Chase, I can't afford to—"

"I'll take care of that. There's a direct flight out of Dulles tomorrow morning which will get you here in a couple of hours. You can be back Sunday night."

Her eyes sprung open to stare at the ceiling. She remembered that feeling, when you could pick up a phone or open a web browser and just buy what you wanted. For a brief second she felt the shallow, envious tug from her previous life, but it was quickly doused by reality.

"I'm not sure I can," she said now.

A beat passed, then, "I understand."

"Chase, I don't—"

"It's okay, Vanessa. You don't have to."

No, she didn't. But she understood what it meant for him to ask and that meant something to her.

"No, I want to do this, Chase. Let me make a few calls," she said.

He paused, then said, "You sure?"

"Yes. Call me back in ten."

She hung up with a click then dialed her sister's cell number. "Jules."

"Ness! We were just talking about you!"

Vanessa frowned. "Who's 'we'?"

"Oh, Mom and Dad and some client of theirs. We're at Citronelle. Have you seen this place? It's gorgeous!"

"No, I haven't. Listen, when are you going back to L.A.?"

"A week Saturday. Why?"

Vanessa bit her lip. "How would you like to spend some quality time with your nieces?"

* * *

When Chase finally hung up he paused, the phone in his hand as he stared out into the black night from his patio window. Any minute now, it would hit—the tight gut, the pounding head, the sweat. His body was a pretty accurate prewarning system and he'd gotten adept at listening to the signs of doubt, trusting his instincts when his head failed.

This time, however, nothing happened. Still, he waited a full ten minutes, engrossed in the view, before he finally placed the phone on the desk.

He'd made the right decision.

Mitch ran a ranch, coped with Sam's illness, plus dealt with Jess running out on him. So much crap in his life, yet he remained strong, unbending, resolute. It was the kind of strength Chase sensed in Vanessa, the kind of strength he wished he had. The kind of strength that faltered every time he started to tell Sam he had the last Charlie Jack book. Just thinking of reading that story aloud, alone, knowing it was the beginning of the end, engulfed him in a huge wave of sadness.

Did that make him selfish for wishing Vanessa was with him, to channel some of that sadness?

Without her physical distraction, he'd found himself totally focused on their conversations these past few days. Vanessa not only revealed a very smart mind, but also, to his surprise, a wicked sense of humor. He'd actually loosened up, even caught his grinning reflection in the glass door once or twice. Pretty soon, hanging up had become an annoyance and he'd spent the next day looking forward to that night's call, then the next, like some giddy, smitten kid.

They might have started out talking about normal stuff, but they also veered off course, and that's when it had turned weird.

Weird in a "dangerous, uncharted territory" way.

Chase had never really gotten the hang of flirting. As a teenager he'd been too embarrassed and lacking confidence. Then, as an adult, women had seemed perfectly okay with verbalizing exactly what they wanted from him. Frankly, he'd appreciated the no-nonsense honesty. But this was different. He and Vanessa talked—seemingly innocuous topics—yet a subtle undercurrent tightened his body and sent his heartbeat galloping every time.

Like those two kisses.

He shoved his hands in his pockets, rocking back on his heels.

And now Vanessa was coming here. With Mitch's approval, Chase had not only invited her to the Mac-D Ranch, but also into a private part of his life.

He stilled, squeezing his eyes shut for good measure, but the only emotion chomping away in his belly was nervous anticipation.

He wanted to see her again. Damn, was actually eager for it. A need had taken shape inside, growing until it had urged him into action. An action that was so out of character that he'd second-guessed his decision up until the very moment he'd asked Vanessa to join him.

He scowled at his reflection before turning away.

Interesting that now, after all these years, he'd succumbed to a lust that dictated his actions and went against all those years of self-preservation.

No, it wasn't just lust. Dunbar had obviously rewritten parts of the story with Erin and Heather in mind, so including Vanessa in this, giving her the opportunity to read those scenes in advance, before the book exploded into the stores, was the right thing to do.

Chase always did the right thing.

Nine

"You could have brought Erin and Heather," Chase said for the third time since he'd picked her up from the airport.

"I didn't think that would've been appropriate, considering."

He paused. "No," he finally admitted, his hands twisting on the steering wheel as they hurtled north along the cracked asphalt road. "You're right."

"And my sister wanted to spend some time with them. Stella's on hand if there's a problem." She stared out the window, at the scrub and wooden fence posts passing by at great speed. "I've never seen a real working ranch before."

"What about Colorado?"

"We were in Breckenridge, in the winter," she reminded him. "You're talking ski resorts and private chalets, not a hundred head of cattle."

"Try for a few thousand and you'll be closer. There's the house," he added, nodding through the windscreen.

A massive wooden sign across the graveled drive heralded The Mac-D Ranch followed by a double-looped M and D brand. As they took the turn, a myriad of fences flanked the road and finally, at the end of the long driveway sat the homestead. It was a weathered dark brick single-story affair, with a wrap-around porch, huge patio windows and a weathered green roof. Past that, past more fences, she saw an array of barns and sheds, a huge truck and some gathering cattle.

As they pulled to a stop, a man emerged from a nearby shed and came to meet them, his long, loping stride and easy rolling gait a perfect match for his rangy body and broad shoulders. A real cowboy from the top of his battered Stetson, plaid shirt and sun-bleached jeans, all the way down to his dusty work boots.

"Mitch, this is Vanessa Partridge. Vanessa, Mitchell O'Connor."

He was shorter and broader than Chase, with tanned skin that came from working the land. He swept the hat off his head, wiped a hand on his jeans and offered it with a smile. "Ma'am. Pleased to meet you."

"Please, call me Vanessa. And thank you for letting me visit."

"No problem." He slapped his hat against one thigh. "Plenty of room in the house. Sam's always happy to have visitors."

"How's he doing?" Vanessa tentatively asked.

"Oh, about the same." Mitch's smile faltered for a second before he caught himself. "Chase'll show you to your room, if that's okay. I'll be along as soon as I wrap up here."

"Okay." She gave what she hoped was an encouraging smile as Chase took her bag from the car.

The living room was spotless, with minimal furniture and soft blue painted walls. The open-plan kitchen attached to it housed loads of counter space, a large range and an equally massive fridge.

"You've got the room on the left." Chase indicated the long hall with her bag. "Mine's next door."

"And Sam's?"

"At the other side of the house, along with Olivia's—his nurse—and Mitch's. The bathroom's there—" he nodded as they passed "—and the laundry."

He got to her room and placed her bag on the floor. "I'll see you in the kitchen."

She took in the room's contents—perfectly made double bed, a small bookcase, writing desk next to a pair of sliding doors that opened onto the patio.

When she turned, Chase was still standing in the doorway with a strange, unreadable expression.

"Thank you," he said softly.

"You're welcome. Chase, I—"

He frowned, shaking his head. "You don't have to say anything."

But she wanted to. A hundred questions lay impatiently on her tongue, ready to throw out there. Yet she was pretty sure this wasn't the time or place for airing her insecurities.

So instead, she said, "Okay," and let him go.

For now.

After she unpacked, she made her way to the kitchen. Chase had prepared a huge pitcher of iced tea and was working at filling a battered old percolator with water for coffee, when Mitch walked in the door.

Chase glanced up with a frown. "I thought Tom was due today?"

"He only comes in twice a week."

"But I—"

"Now, Chase, don't go getting your britches in a knot." Mitch stomped his feet on the mat at the back door. "I don't need a cook on call and Olivia fixes all Sam's meals, so there's really no need."

"And where is she now?"

"Had to run into town to do a few chores."

Chase chewed that over, then said, "This thing with Tom—"

"It's just me," Mitch countered. "Makes no sense wasting your money on one mouth. And anyway—" he tossed his hat onto the scarred kitchen table "—Tom freezes enough meals to last until next time."

With that, he walked off down the hall, his boots clomping

on the bare wooden floors. The creak of a door sounded, followed by an overly cheerful "Hey, buddy! How are you doing? Have you met Chase's friend yet?"

"Come on," Chase said, and gently nudged her out of the kitchen.

Vanessa crossed the threshold, not knowing what to expect. A sterile room, perhaps, laden with drips and gadgets and high-tech machines. Yes, there were a few machines, and yes, the room was absolutely spotless. But it was also the room of a nine-year-old boy, a boy who apparently loved martial arts, football and Charlie Jack. His walls were plastered with movie posters, Atlanta Falcons items and huge color photocopied covers of Dunbar's books. On the bulletin board over his desk were sketches of familiar scenes: the mythical subterranean world the young Charlie Jack explored in the first book, the final battle with the evil Skulk at the end of book two. Even Skulk Castle, complete with the feisty princess Charlie rescued in book three.

Then her gaze went to the bed and she had to force every single mothering instinct in her body not to cry.

"Hi," Vanessa said, smiling at the pale, bald boy looking so fragile against the well-worn blue flannel sheets, blue veins stark against his translucent skin. "You must be Sam."

"The tubes gave me away, huh?"

She swallowed, heart lurching as her eyes went to Mitch.

"Don't give Vanessa a hard time, dude." Mitch's hand cupped Sam's smooth head lovingly. "She's here as Chase's guest."

"You his girlfriend?" Sam asked.

Chase met her eyes questioningly. Vanessa looked back at Sam and said, "Just a friend."

"Right. You from New York too?"

"Washington."

Sam's face lit up. "They have the Library of Congress. I love libraries. Grandma worked at the Jasper County one, where my dad was born."

"Your dad was born in a library?"

Sam grinned. "No, silly!"

Vanessa grinned back, pulled up a chair and sat beside the bed. "So what do you like best about libraries?"

"Well, the books, of course. There's so many. Awesome. And it's quiet. You always can tell when—"

Chase and Mitch left them to talk, returning to the kitchen and the now-bubbling percolator.

"So," Mitch began when they'd both filled their mugs with steaming coffee. "You got yourself a Perfect."

Chase glanced sharply over the edge of his cup. "What makes you think she's a Perfect?"

"Oh, I dunno—the skin, the clothes, the way she holds herself. Dude—" he swallowed with a grateful gulp "—she's a Perfect."

Chase shook his head. "No, she's not like that. I mean, she's a nursery school teacher. A single mom."

"So what? Bet she's got rich parents and Daddy gave her a car for graduation."

Chase scowled. What the hell was wrong with Mitch? "Her parents are hotshot Washington defense lawyers, but she's not involved in all that. She's different…nice. Funny. Compassionate. Her girls are the cutest kids I've ever seen and she's a good mom. And she cooks. Man, that lamb roast melts in your mouth…" He trailed off as Mitch's goofy grin spread. "You're jerking me around. You son of a—"

"You like her."

"Yeah."

"Chase likes Vaneeeeessaaaaa," Mitch singsonged, his broad smile half hidden behind his coffee mug.

"What are you, twelve?"

"Chase wants to kiss Vaneeeesa." Mitch expertly dodged Chase's swipe. "He wants to marry her. Chase and Vanessa sitting in a tree—"

"You've always been a total goofball, O'Connor." Chase

gave up, instead opting to lean against the counter and stare daggers at his best friend.

"K-I-S-S-I-N-G."

"How on earth your family put up with you, I have no idea."

"Um, Sam says he's tired."

Startled, they both turned to see Vanessa standing at the mouth of the hallway with a worried look.

"He tires easily," Mitch reassured her. "I'll just go and check on him."

"Iced tea? Coffee?" Chase asked as Mitch disappeared.

"Tea sounds great." She watched in silence as he got out a glass, a spoon then sugar.

When he turned back to her, she was sporting a funny kind of half smile.

"This tree we're in… Is it entirely safe?"

"You heard."

She grinned. "Hard not to."

"That's just Mitch—he's always been a clown. Well," he amended, "not lately. In fact, I haven't seen him joke around for months."

"Understandable, given the circumstances." She paused then said hesitantly, "Where's Sam's mother?"

He frowned, anger surging, hardening his heart. "Jess left six months after Sam was first diagnosed."

Her eyes turned sad. "So Mitch's been coping for how long?"

"Nearly two years."

He slid the glass across the counter and she took it, wrapping her fingers around the base but not drinking.

"What kind of mother walks away from her sick child?"

"Someone who obviously can't cope."

"Yes, but…" A frown marred her forehead as she stood there, silently sifting through her thoughts. "It comes with the territory. You're a parent and it's your job to look after your baby. No excuses."

When she finally met his eyes, Chase felt the moment

change. It was as if a kind of mutual purpose had formed around them, one that went deep and strong, right to the very core of their beliefs.

And just like that, something shifted inside.

Vanessa was nothing like what he'd expected. She aroused him, yes, but since he'd met her, she'd been surprising the hell out of him and challenging the boundaries of his teenage prejudices.

She had a fierce determination underneath all that quiet dignity. It told him she'd never be a Jess. She had more depth, more integrity than any other woman he'd known. And she was here, far away from her babies, because Chase had asked her to read to a boy she didn't know.

A manuscript that, given a different outcome, should have been Erin and Heather's.

A deep, strange yearning shot through every muscle, confusing the hell out of him. So, to hide it, he said, "We should start reading as soon as Sam feels up to it."

He caught Vanessa's brief nod before he moved down the hall.

As expected, Sam was thrilled with Chase's surprise and asked that they start on the story right away. Vanessa and Chase had agreed to take turns reading a chapter each, but when it was Vanessa's, Chase found himself so wrapped up in her gentle, melodious rendition, so full of enthusiasm for the story and the magical world of Charlie Jack, that he just wanted to sit back and listen to her read for hours. Instead, after the fourth chapter, he noticed Sam's eyes drooping and called time-out.

Vanessa insisted on cooking dinner despite Mitch's and Chase's protests. In twenty minutes, she'd fixed a potato salad and greens, and three marinated steaks were busy sizzling on the griddle.

"Sam's still sleeping?" Vanessa asked as Mitch strode into the kitchen and headed straight for the fridge.

"Yep," he replied, grabbing a beer from the door, twisting it open then throwing the cap into the sink. She remained silent under his head-to-toe scrutiny, his eyes narrowed as he tapped that bottle absently on his belt buckle.

"Does he sleep a lot?" Vanessa finally asked.

"Yeah. He's always tired these days. Chemo and drugs have pretty much wiped him out."

For once, Vanessa didn't have an acceptable comeback to that. What did you say to a terminal child's father? Sorry just wouldn't cut it, and yet the word still hovered on her tongue. Instead, she swallowed it back down and said softly, "Is Chase with him?"

"Shower." He tilted his head questioningly. "How long have you known Chase?"

"A few weeks."

Mitch's eyebrows shot up. "Hmm."

She went over to turn the steaks. "Is that a good 'hmm' or a bad 'hmm'?"

"Depends. He told me about you."

Vanessa blinked, her face neutral. "And what did he tell you?"

"Who your parents are, where you live, what you do." He paused then added, "Must be tough, raising twins by yourself."

She shrugged. "I manage. You have to."

He nodded. "So what are your intentions toward Chase?"

Her eyes widened at his frankly assessing stare. "You're giving me the talk?"

"Do I need to?"

"Is Chase really that bad a judge of character?" she countered.

Mitch snorted in amusement. "Oh, yeah. In freshman year he couldn't get a date to save himself. Then he filled out, grew up and *bam!* Women falling over themselves to talk to him."

"That's good to know." She smiled wryly.

"Hey, I say it like it is. Getting women isn't a problem. Getting a *decent* one, well…"

She began to arrange the plates on the table, replaying

Thursday night's conversation in her head. "So he had a few girlfriends in college."

"I wouldn't call them that." Mitch took a swig of beer then glanced to the door. "He's not told you this himself, then."

"Just that he wasn't the jock type."

Mitch's beer nearly spluttered through his nose. After he finished coughing and wiping his mouth, he began to laugh. "God, understatement of the century! No, he was definitely *not* the jock type. We were both textbook nerds until about nineteen." He put the beer on the table and took up the cutlery, placing it beside the plates.

They set the table in silence until Vanessa finally said, "So you must've known his parents."

Mitch froze for a moment, shooting her a look, before heading over to the cabinet. "Yeah, I knew them."

"And?"

"They were jerks."

"That doesn't really explain anything."

Mitch sighed, placing two glasses firmly on the table. "White trailer trash with a lot of money. His father was a real piece of work, a smooth charmer. Eyeballed any female who walked into his store. Chase's mom, on the other hand, was high maintenance—lots of tight skirts, high heels and makeup." He finished with the glasses and placed his hands wide on the table. "Two stupid, juvenile people who produced a genius like Chase."

"Genius?"

"He was the recipient of the Sterling Scholarship, a private, internationally renowned scheme funded by a bunch of anonymous donors. They award something like ten in the entire world. You get to choose your college if you pass the tough entrance exam and three rounds of interviews."

Wow. For one second the enormity of Chase's intelligence was a terrible, daunting thing, until she remembered the challenges he'd faced and what he'd had to overcome.

"So his folks fought a lot."

"Yeah. They had major trust issues and argued nearly every week." He took another swig of beer and leaned his hip on the table. "And not just privately, either."

"Ah." Vanessa winced.

"Yep. Not only was Chase the son of Mad Max Harrington—the loud crazy guy screaming at you on TV, trying to sell you a bed—" he made a distasteful face "—but his folks played out their little 'you're cheating on me' drama in the main street nearly every weekend. You could damn near set your watch by it."

Vanessa swallowed, her heart aching for the boy Chase had been.

"He copped a lot of crap for it at school." Mitch shook his head. "Bullied by the Perfects—"

"Perfects?"

"The jocks and their girlfriends. You know the type—latest clothes, cool phones, flashy cars…" He paused, and his face flushed.

"Total snobs who thought everyone was beneath them?"

When Mitch nodded, Vanessa realized everything was finally starting to make sense. That night at the library, he'd called her perfect. But he'd really meant "Perfect."

That's why he'd mistrusted her on sight—because she reminded him of a painful past he'd spent most of his life trying to escape. And yet…he'd opened up to her. Invited her into this part of his life. That meant something. At the very least, it meant he was beginning to trust her. And that was important, more important than she'd first realized.

After Mitch went to take a shower, Vanessa was left alone with the calming routine of cooking, so of course, her thoughts returned to Chase.

The attraction was a given. He could charm the panties off a nun, her grandmother would say. Choking back a snort of laughter, she turned to strain the greens. She'd also have a lot to say about her current fascination with Chase Harrington.

He revealed himself to her in little pieces: in conversation, in everything he chose not to say, and how he responded to life's crises. Despite her initial thought—that Chase would be a fabulous way to pass the time with no strings—she found herself becoming more and more drawn to him.

And just as if she'd imagined him, he appeared at the door, clean shaven and dressed in jeans and sweater, his hair sticking up in still-damp spikes.

"Need a hand?" He smiled.

She felt the flush deep inside, warming everything. In silence she thrust out the potato salad before finally finding her voice. "On the table?"

"Sure." When he strode over, his bare feet padding softly on the wooden floors, she gulped in a breath. Chase in his suit and tie always held massive appeal, but now, in jeans, barefoot and smelling of soap and shaving cream...

Devastating. Droolworthy.

He took the bowl and turned to the table and despite where she was, despite why she was here, a part of her still wanted to rip his clothes off.

That was the powerful pull of Chase Harrington—not his money or influence or even his whip-smart mind. And amazingly, he had no idea of his own attraction. If he did...damn, the man was *the* most brilliant actor ever.

And you've fallen for him, haven't you? Despite all that non-analyzing, the "ooh, a no-strings fling," she'd gone and fallen for Chase Harrington. She'd already committed by accepting his non-date and since then, everything she'd learned about him had only sucked her in deeper. Today had been the final step.

She sighed, watching him take the iced tea from the fridge and place it on the table.

So she just needed to get through this weekend without doing something dumb, like deciding she could fix him. Her experience with Dunbar had taught her quite definitively that relationships built on that were not only stupid but self-destructive. And anyway, who was she to say Chase needed to be fixed? He seemed perfectly happy with the person he was.

Who was she to judge his deeply held beliefs on relationships and marriage and how that impacted his life? However skewed she thought those beliefs were, they had shaped his life, given him the passion and drive to make him into the success he was today.

Yet for all their similarities, their blossoming trust and the obvious chemistry, could she ignore the fact that pursuing something further with Chase would ultimately end in heartbreak?

Ten

After dinner Mitch went to check on Sam while Chase made coffee. When everything was prepared, he gestured to the door. "Want to go outside?"

Vanessa nodded and they took their coffee out on the patio, settling on the front steps as the sun displayed a glorious sunset over the mountains.

They sipped in silence, enjoying the view and the still evening, punctuated by the occasional lowing of cattle.

"I have to say, Mitch's handling this really well," Vanessa finally said. "I can't imagine what it must be like for him."

Chase gave a brief, grim smile. "Oh, there've been bad days. But he's also had a few years to process it. And Mitch has always been an unflappable guy. Give him a problem and he jumps right on in to fix it."

But he couldn't. They both fell silent, each thinking the same thing.

"There's no other family around to help?" Vanessa queried.

"His dad died when he was two, and his mom retired and moved to Nevada. His father-in-law died a few years back. And his brothers and sisters are all out of state. Anyway, there's not much they can do. The ranch runs like clockwork and Mitch has all the help he needs."

She took a sip of coffee. "How did you two meet? Mitch told me a bit about—"

Chase mumbled something under his breath.

"Sorry?" Vanessa frowned.

"I said, Mitch never did learn to shut his mouth."

"What's wrong with talking to me?"

"Because my private life isn't a conversation piece."

She took exception to his snippy tone. "Who do you think I'm going to tell?"

Their gazes clashed until Chase broke away to stare off into the rapidly darkening night. He scowled into his hands, absently rubbing a thumb over his knuckles. "Fine. You want to know? I met Mitch at the Jasper County library." He glanced over his shoulder, through the huge patio doors to the kitchen table where Mitch was frowning over the mail. "His mom was the librarian and he went to another school. We just clicked." His expression suddenly softened with a small memory-laden smile. "Man, we were inseparable. After school, summer vacation…" He gave a small huff of amusement. "I practically lived at his place. It was crowded, always full of kids, and his mother was awesome. I loved it."

"What about your parents? Did they mind that you spent so much time away from home?"

He leaned forward, resting his elbows on his knees, and stared at his feet. "They didn't care."

"But surely—"

His face tightened. "If I wasn't around, they had nothing to bargain with."

That did it. Despite her stern talking-to earlier, she couldn't shake this desperate need to understand why Chase was the way he was, to help him smooth over those old scars. It was the very least she could do, when he'd invited her into his world.

But she had to exercise caution, otherwise he'd shut her down.

"Did you guys go to college together?"

Chase nodded. "Until Mitch dropped out."

Before she could ask, he continued. "Jess got pregnant. So he did the right thing, got married then came back here to run her dad's ranch."

It was telling, the choice Mitch had made. It meant he was an honorable guy, accepting his responsibilities no matter what the personal consequence. It said a lot about Chase's character, too, as Mitch's best friend.

She suspected they were similar in that respect: it took a strong man, one with a lot of integrity, to take such a major life detour.

Chase was nothing like his awful upbringing. *He* was definitely not a guy who'd walk out on his pregnant girlfriend.

She sighed.

The dark evening enveloped them and they shared it in silence, each wrapped in their own private memories as they sat, side by side, separated on the porch steps by a foot of cold night. Vanessa suppressed a shiver beneath her sheepskin jacket, wrapping her hands around the rapidly cooling coffee. Chase had been more open with her in the last few hours than he had the entire time she'd known him. To say she was hopefully optimistic was an understatement.

After a while of silence, she said softly, "Our history is not that different, you know. We were both forced to grow up quickly because of bad parents."

Chase frowned, marring the perfect line of his profile, before he shot her a sideways glance. "Your mother didn't drag you downtown to your father's store, then stand in the middle of the street screaming at him."

Her heart lurched. "Is that what happened?"

"Yeah. My mother wasn't big on trust—any time a woman smiled at my dad she thought he was having an affair. Sure, the guy was always chatting up the women but as far as I knew that was it. And of course, my mom was always tarting herself up and flirting with the customers. So they'd yell at each other for ages, unable to prove anything, dragging up the same old arguments over and over, while I died of embarrassment and tried to disappear against the brickwork."

"That's awful."

His face twisted into a half grimace. "'Chase,' she always used to say, 'men are pigs. You can't trust them.' Yet she stayed with my father because 'he provides for me,'" he air quoted with a scowl.

Oh, boy. No wonder Chase's perception of marriage and relationships was so distorted. She'd have trouble trusting people too, with an upbringing like that.

"Mine were always working," Vanessa said now. "I must've been about six when we had a parents' day at school. I automatically asked the nanny." Her soft laugh felt dry in her throat. "We had the standard nanny, then a housekeeper for ages, ferrying us to requisite music lessons, tennis, ballet. Every day it was school, then extracurricular activities. On the weekends, study and educational excursions. Like keeping busy was a competitive sport or something. We always had to be productive, have a *purpose.* I've always known their careers took first priority. Juliet, my sister, came second." She smiled faintly. "She was the charming one, the socialite, the budding lawyer-to-be. Dad had her pegged for his practice, but she went and became a divorce lawyer. And until recently, she'd been a major disappointment, apparently. Although—" her grin faded "—not as much as I am."

He snorted, shaking his head. "I just don't get that. You have a good job, two happy, healthy babies…"

"Ah, but it infuriates my father that I'm not 'living up to my potential,'" she quoted. "After everything they put into my education and my upbringing, all the strings they pulled, I'm now wasting it in a low-paid job. And let's not forget, no worthy man would want a wife who already had kids with a secret lover."

"Is that what they told you?"

"In more colorful language, but yes." After nearly two years she still couldn't recall her parents' fury and disappointment without her chest tightening. Her father's displeasure had been explosively palpable, but it was her mother who'd thrown the barb that had stuck, planting insidious seeds of doubt. "Apparently I'm damaged goods now and will never find a man."

Chase shook his head. "That's crazy."

"No, that's my parents."

"God, spare us from our parents' bizarre expectations."

She shot him a glance. "What did yours want you to do?"

"Besides stay out of jail? Oh, I thought about doing it just to piss them off," he added with a thin smile. "But no. They told me I'd take over the family business. I just wanted to get the hell out of there."

"So you went to Harvard."

"On a scholarship. They refused to pay."

The elite Sterling Scholarship with only ten recipients in the entire world. "I can't picture you being satisfied with an average life in a small town."

"Really?"

"Yes. You seem much more ambitious than that." She turned her hips so she was now facing him, placing her now-cold cup to one side before giving him her full attention. "There's this buzz about you, an energy. I've seen the way people are around you—the men all want your opinion, and they actually listen when you talk. And the women…"

A skeptical half smile curved his lips. "What about the women?"

"They just want to take your clothes off."

His sudden shot of laughter frosted in the cold air, surprising them both. It just went to show that in the most desperate of times, there could still be moments of relief, she realized. But it still felt sort of wrong how much she enjoyed watching his eyes crease, the way that throaty sexy laugh warmed all her cold places.

"And what about you, Vanessa?" When he leaned in, his breath charging the space between them, the moment turned deadly serious.

She sucked in air, the cold a welcome shock to her senses. "Don't ask me a question you don't want to know the answer to."

"I never make assumptions."

"Okay." With her heart hammering in her throat, she leaned in a little bit more, until their mouths were barely even a breath apart, until she could feel his heat on the curve of her bottom lip. "I want to take your clothes off, too."

Surprise, amusement, then arousal—all three flashed across Chase's face, until the shadowed depths of his eyes seemed to burn her inside. "I want you to kiss me, Chase."

She needn't have asked—his mouth was already there.

It was just how a kiss should have been: all soft and full of uncertainty. Her eyes fluttered closed as the moment flowed over her, building a gentle swell of warmth in her blood, firing her belly. His lips tentatively explored hers, at first tender, then as she kissed him back, with greater force.

He tasted of coffee, heat and pure maleness. He smelled of soap, home and desire.

Her mouth parted, welcoming him in and with a groan he accepted her invitation, his tongue tasting, tangling. She could hear his breath as it quickened, knowing hers matched and thrilling at the sudden knowledge that she was the cause of his excitement.

He excited her, too, in ways she'd never thought she could be. Just talking to him, being with him, wasn't enough. She wanted to touch and kiss him, have him do the same, then get naked and share herself.

So what if there were still so many facets to Chase Harrington she'd yet to uncover? There were obviously things he wanted to keep private and she could understand that. The important thing right now was she wanted him and he wanted her. And frankly, she was sick of living like a nun. She needed passion in her life. She missed it.

And Chase needed something else to focus on than the harsh reality of his visit, even if it was something as simple as a kiss.

She felt his hand come up to cup her cheek, the palm searing her skin, branding her before the kiss became deeper.

Did she say simple? Everything blurred—the cold, the night, where they were. Nothing existed except him and the crazy things he was doing to her—forcing her breath from her lungs, sending her blood pounding. Making every inch ache with desire.

"Vanessa," he murmured against her mouth.

"Mmm."

"I want you." He came in for another kiss, this time taking her bottom lip between his and sucking gently. All she could do was groan her consent as his fingers dived into her hair and angled her head for better access.

This was…excruciatingly, mind-numbingly good. Damn, she would combust right there on the spot if he kept on going. But there was no way she wanted him to stop.

"What…are…we—" she managed to get out between breaths and kisses, until the porch door slid open and they both nearly jumped out of their skin.

"Sorry to interrupt, but Sam's awake," Mitch said from the doorway, his nonchalance hiding a barely suppressed grin. "And he's asking for you both."

Reality came crashing in, slamming her back down to earth. With a tight breath, Vanessa nodded and got to her feet before finally glancing at Chase.

Everything plummeted.

He'd accused her of wearing a mask, but that was exactly what he had on right now. Worse, it was that awful, tight "I have total control of my emotions" expression, one she'd only caught glimpses of but had grown to hate nonetheless. It looked so secure that she wondered if she really did know him at all.

As she followed him down the hall, his rigid shoulders and straight back a painful thing to follow, an awful thought occurred. What if, after they finished reading the book, Chase chose to stay with that lonely, "nothing can touch me" mask? That just like his past, he let this tragedy scar him?

Some people let it take over, living only half a life with the pain a festering wound just below the surface.

It'd break her heart if he did.

They finished reading *The Last Ninja* on Saturday night, just as the first cold drops of rain began to fall.

After Sam had fallen asleep, Vanessa had excused herself to her room, desperate to be alone with her confusing thoughts.

Dunbar's familiar scrawl revealed way more than he'd ever admitted to her. It was strange, having his vulnerability written down for anyone to see. Apparently, he had been wracked with a multitude of doubts about the direction of his characters – were they too dark? Too vengeful? What kind of message was he sending to kids? And then the big one that affected her most of all: every time he changed his characters to "Erin" or "Heather" he'd put in a question mark. At the end of the story, it had been explained in the notes summary.

Ask V.

Is this what he'd wanted to talk to her about—to get her approval? And would she have given it?

She sighed and rolled to her side, punching the pillow as she recalled their breakup, his last phone call and her anger following that.

And now she at least had an answer of sorts. Dylan had walked out but this proved he'd been thinking about his children, honoring them by writing two strong, fearless characters in his final book. It was a wonderful yet ultimately sad moment and not for the first time, Vanessa wished things could have turned out different.

Yet if they had, she'd never have met Chase.

With another sigh, she pushed the past from her mind and refocused on the present.

Chase.

They hadn't revisited that kiss and even though Vanessa remained awake for two more excruciatingly slow hours, wondering, hoping, Chase had remained absent from her bed.

Which is how it should be, she chastised herself in the morning, her face warm with shame. She was there for Sam, not to have convenient sex with Chase.

On Sunday morning Vanessa said her goodbyes to the O'Connors, torn between wanting to stay and support Chase yet aching for her reality, having her girls in her arms, touching their chubby faces and breathing in their clean, baby scent.

Thick loaded silence accompanied their drive to the airport, both she and Chase wrapped up in the significance of her departure.

I love you.

She wanted to say the words, fill the car with hope instead of loss, dispel that pain hovering behind Chase's controlled expression and tight mouth. She wanted to make it all okay for him.

No, she couldn't throw that out there right now, not when his troubled blue eyes gave her pause, a vast and terrifying sadness that stopped her breath. She could see the toll it took on him to hide it all.

After Chase put her on the plane with his lingering kiss still burning on her cheek, her heart felt as if someone had cut it out and stomped all over it.

She buckled up, sucked in a deep breath and let the takeoff throw her back into the plush first-class seat.

Even now, she missed him. She wanted him.

Heaven help her, she loved him. She loved that he was so tender, so sweet with Sam. She loved that he'd brought joy into the boy's life without a thought to the material cost. Watching him listen, rapt and wide-eyed as they read the story made her heart contract all over again. She loved that Chase gave of himself, choosing to be with Sam and Mitch even though it was obviously a deeply private time for them. Sam's mother may have walked out, but Chase was there for them, not just as moral support but to ease the financial burden, too.

She loved him so furiously that it damn well scared her to

death. Because she just knew he would break her heart. And she'd never recover from it.

Yet what choice did she have but to willingly follow that stubborn heart of hers?

The clouds outside her window thinned and soon they were gliding in the bright, blue sky, high above everything.

She'd refused to let her experience with Dylan color her opinions of love, romance and the male species. Yet she'd not gone out of her way to pursue those things, preferring to stay at home with her girls.

Had it really been nearly two years? No holding hands, no intimate touches, no morning kisses. If truth be told, Dylan hadn't been big on those things, anyway. She'd always felt a little ripped off, even if she was content to bask in his starry glow.

With a sigh, Vanessa reached for the newspaper in the seat pocket. She had to stop thinking about this so much. It would make her crazy if she let it.

Yes, she'd had her fair share of awful moments, put her faith and trust in people who didn't deserve it. But she couldn't go through life like that anymore. She couldn't, for her girls' sake.

You just need to be there for Chase, if and when he needs you. The rest...well, you can sort that out later.

Decision made, she unfolded the paper, glanced at the headlines—Waverly's had hit the front page again—and settled in for the flight.

A week. Seven whole days and she'd not heard from Chase.

She'd planned to call him the day after she'd left, but Erin had developed a fever and she was up and down for the next two nights, checking and rechecking her temperature, administering baby aspirin and lying in bed with half an ear open for sounds of restlessness. And during the day she had no time to think of anything except for the kids and her work.

Sunday saw her exhausted and planning an early night until Chase turned up on her doorstep.

Everything about him was rigid, from his shoulders and

back, to his firm jaw and stance. Wound up to the point of impossible tightness.

Oh, no.

"I thought you should know. Sam died last Monday." His voice was bleached of emotion.

When she gasped, his jaw clenched and his eyes slid from hers to a point past her shoulder.

"Oh, Chase…" Anguish brimmed to the surface, threatening to spill over. "Come inside."

"I can't. I have a meeting in an hour, then I'm leaving for New York in the morning."

"Where…where are you staying?"

"The Benson near Capitol Hill."

"Chase." She nudged the door wider. "Cancel your meeting and come in."

The raw pain in his eyes nearly broke her.

"I…" He glanced away and she could see his jaw working, then his throat, as he cleared it.

"Chase?" She reached out for his arm. "Are you…?"

His hard glare, combined with the distance he put between them as he stepped back, stopped her cold.

"Don't ask if I'm okay because I'm damn-well not." He dragged in a deep breath, swept a hand across his eyes. "This was a mistake. I shouldn't have come."

"No, I—"

"I've gotta go."

Before she could say another word, he turned on his heel and strode away, leaving her more alone than she'd been before.

Later that night, after Vanessa put on a brave face for Erin and Heather then cried in her room, she sat brooding on the couch, a glass of wine in hand and a clean piece of paper on her knee.

She was so very grateful for her girls, for her life, imperfect though it was. She'd had her heart broken, but still she'd pulled herself together. And now, here was the bundle of complication that was Chase Harrington. A spanner in the works who'd inadvertently made her believe that love could happen again, and in the most unlikely places.

Her heart wrenched, a painful, bittersweet feeling as she halfheartedly put in the final folds of her figure.

His rejection cut deep. After everything they'd shared, everything he'd revealed to her, he still didn't trust her to see him at his most vulnerable. Her heart ached for the boy who'd first learned that horrible life lesson all those years ago.

She tapped her fingers on the table, absently drumming out a rhythm.

It wasn't right, leaving him like this. Maybe she'd come into Chase's life for a reason. Maybe he had to be shown you shouldn't let the past eat away at you, and that the world wasn't filled with cold, hard people.

Maybe they were each other's second chances.

She gently placed the origami on the table, critically assessing her work. The sharp lines and intricate folds revealed a perfect, tiny miniature of One Madison Park. Chase's apartment.

With a sigh she tossed the rest of the paper on the table.

What was Chase doing now? Getting drunk at a bar? Or brooding alone in his hotel suite, dwelling on a bunch of what-ifs he couldn't change? Was he blaming himself? Was there something he could've done, a treatment or drugs he could've provided? Or was he racked with survivor's guilt?

He shouldn't be alone after something like this. She couldn't bear either scenario, imagining him trying to cope with the sense of futility that death brought.

Vanessa sprung to her feet, plunked the wineglass on the table and went for the phone.

With her thumbnail flicking her front tooth she dialed the familiar number, jigging one leg impatiently as it rang.

"Stella? I need your help."

Half an hour later, she took the elevator up to Chase's hotel room, the shiny mirrored walls reflecting the determined lines on her face, the serious glint in her eye. Beyond that, she barely had time to notice that her hair was a mess and she'd not put on any lipstick. With a dismayed groan she dug in her handbag, came up with an old tube of strawberry gloss and quickly applied it as the doors swished open onto the top floor.

She sighed at her hair, smoothed it back into its ponytail, frowned then removed the tie. After a gentle tousle she shrugged. Too late now.

She stepped out into the corridor, heading toward the door at the far end. It was an imposing double-locked affair, barring entry to all.

Just like Chase, she thought, her soft footfalls engulfed by plush carpeting. Her heart hammered away, full of doubt and hope as she chewed on her fingernail, biting it down to a painful nub.

Damn. She quickly dropped her hand, shoved it in her coat pocket and took a deep, steadying breath.

It was all or nothing now. She pressed a palm to her chest, her heart beating way too fast. A thin trickle of sweat made a track down her lower back and she bit her lip, a foot in both camps for one indecisive second.

Then she knocked on the door.

Eleven

Chase was halfway through the contents of the liquor cabinet, slumped in the leather couch and glaring through the wide plasma screen that currently displayed the news.

His phone vibrated again, the fourth time in ten minutes, but he ignored it. There was a massive hole in his heart that no amount of alcohol or self-flagellation could fill. Yes, he'd prepared himself for the moment, had gone over and over it in his head, way too knowledgeable about the realities of the disease and what everyone could expect when Sam's time inevitably came.

And yet he'd been woefully unprepared for the actual reality of it all. Hell, Mitch had held it together better than him, even encouraged him to return to New York after the funeral.

Stay busy, keep working. Occupy your mind.

Of all the pointless, terrible things that had happened in his life, this had to top it all.

And oh, the irony. It had taken one boy for him to realize how much of a caricature he'd become. He was severely out of touch with everything and everyone, operating in the alter-

nate reality of his billion-dollar life. He hadn't known how to
be real anymore.

But thanks to Sam, he'd changed. His quest had led him
to Vanessa and all the amazing possibilities he never thought
would be offered to him. She and her small, self-sufficient
family had showed him what was important.

Ah. Vanessa. Red hair, green eyes and a seductive mouth
that rocked his world.

Walking away from her had taken every ounce of his control, every single shred of strength. But he had to.

Seeing her face filled with so much sadness, so much pity
for him had nearly sliced him open, spilling emotion right
there on the floor. He'd been horrified by the prick of tears
behind his eyes.

He never cried in public, not after that last mortifying time
in junior high. The chanting, the cruel taunts… Christ, he'd
never let go of that, would he?

Yet here he was, fifteen all over again, struggling to hold
everything together, to force the tears, the emotion and fear
back inside, to show no one vulnerability or weakness.

Thank God she hadn't seen him like that.

It had taken supreme willpower to stuff everything back behind those walls before they had a chance to crumble. But he'd
done it, even as her eyes had welled and she'd reached for him.

Breaking down in front of her, losing it, was something she
didn't need to see. Control defined him: emotion did not. If he
couldn't keep it together, he was good to no one.

Deep in brooding silence, he barely heard the knock on the
door until the tapping became a firm pounding. Gritting his
teeth, he muttered a dozen colorful words under his breath before settling on the least offensive.

"Go away!"

The knocking stopped.

"Chase," came the muffled reply. "It's Vanessa. Open the
door."

With a groan, he ran a hand over his face, ending at his stubbled chin. The rough hairs jabbed into his palm, a reminder that he'd not shaved in a couple of days, that he was in desperate need of a shower and that, strangely, he couldn't give a damn.

"Chase," she repeated firmly. "I'm going to keep knocking until you open this door."

He cursed aloud now, lurched to his feet then swayed as the alcohol hit.

Goddammit. After a couple of slow, heavy blinks and a deep breath, he made his way to the door, swallowing thickly all the way.

"Go home, Vanessa," he growled through the door.

"No."

"Go. Home."

"Open the door, Chase."

"Dammit, I don't want to see you!"

After a brief silence, Chase shoved his eye to the peephole. Had she taken the hint?

No.

"Well, I need to see you," she said, glaring right into the hole.

Arrrrrgh! With all the frustration behind his groan, he yanked the door open.

And looked straight into a pair of beautiful green eyes, fixed firm and steady on him.

The anger died on his lips.

Vanessa sniffed. He smelled of expensive bourbon and despair, his grief something she could almost touch. It was a barrier keeping her at bay.

She swallowed, bolstered her courage and refused to let that give her pause. This was her fighting for what she wanted. For what she sensed he couldn't say outright.

"This is not a good time for me, Vanessa," he muttered, one hand sweeping through his hair as he glared at the floor. "Go home to your children."

"I think you need me more."

He stilled, raking her with his red-rimmed gaze. "Really."

Before she had a chance to blink, he'd yanked her inside, slammed the door behind him and shoved her up against the wall. "And what do you know about what I really need?"

"I know you shouldn't be alone. Let me be with you."

Everything about him, the tone of his voice, his granite expression, the way he crowded her, all screamed keep out. He was trying so hard to push her away and she could see the war he waged inside: the air was thick with it.

Worry crawled up her throat but she forced it back down.

"You want to be with me?" he snarled. "Perfect Vanessa Partridge with her old-world money and her highbrow family wants to be with *me?*"

"Chase…"

"Yeah, me. Fat, ugly Chase Harrington from Obscure, Texas." He pressed into her, his face so close not even a breath could escape, the air sweet with the scent of bourbon. "The geeky son of Mad Max Harrington, whose parents threatened divorce every weekend—to the delight of the entire town—then had loud make-up sex in the nearest hotel room while I died of shame every. Single. Time. That's who you want to be with?"

Oh, Lord, he was killing her. Tears prickled behind her eyes, his anguish laced with self-disgust breaking her heart into a million tiny shards. Through her coat, beneath his thin shirt, his pulse raced, his breath deep and angry, and she swallowed, refusing to succumb to the danger in those flame-blue eyes. He was trying to push her away and dammit, she would not let him.

She shifted her feet even though he had practically every other inch of her body pinned.

"I'm so sorry, Chase," she said slowly. "I'm so sorry that your past made you so distrustful. And I'm sorry about Sam. It's an awful thing to happen to a child, let alone a child who's close to you. But he was terminal. Nothing you could've done would've saved his life. You know that."

He glared then suddenly pulled back, taking that searing heat with him. "No, I don't know that," he said.

She'd frowned. "Surely you can't—"

"Maybe if I'd been involved in his life instead of ignoring Mitch's calls, the disease could've been caught earlier. I mean, what the hell is all that money for if you can't make a difference?"

"But you did make a difference."

"Yeah. I read him a *book*," he spat out, every word lashed with contempt.

It infuriated her. "Don't do that. Don't you dare make out like you did nothing. Sam had a wish and you made that come true. To say it was less than that is not only belittling his memory—it's also an insult to Mitch. If you want to yell and scream, do it. If you want to get drunk, do that too. But do *not* say that you did nothing. I think it's probably the best thing you've done in your entire life."

When he said nothing, she deliberately softened her expression and took a step forward, forcing herself to be the one in his face this time. "Chase, I'm here now. I lost someone, too. I want to help you."

When his nostrils flared she sucked in a sharp breath, sensing danger as the mood shifted. His eyes darkened, then his frown, but she held her ground when he took that last step and closed the gap.

Barely nothing separated them. Not a breath, nor a gasp, nor a heartbeat. But when she moved in to kiss him, he leaned back and all she could feel on her lips was the tense air between them.

She didn't move. Didn't breathe. Just waited, hope roaring through her veins as she held his troubled gaze in hers.

"I wish I could make it right for you," she said softly, not trusting her voice above a whisper. "I wish I could help."

He groaned, a sound so full of frustration that it made her want to wrap her arms around him and draw his pain into her body.

"You are. I want—" he took her in, devouring her with his eyes "—you. I've wanted you from the very start."

Then his mouth dipped and he was almost touching hers, almost but not quite. She breathed nothing—felt nothing—but him. He surrounded her, filled her.

Then suddenly they were kissing and everything else just disappeared. His lips slid against hers, hard and demanding, and she took it, let him bruise her mouth, grip the back of her neck and angle her head so he could go deeper.

He pressed against her, backing them up until they hit the wall and she had no place left to go.

She wouldn't want to anyway. Vanessa had imagined this moment for a long time, him kissing her, his tongue thrusting and tangling with hers while his manhood throbbed insistently between them. It had hijacked her waking moments, snuck into her dreams, accompanied even the most mundane of tasks.

And now she could think of nothing else.

"Take me to bed, Chase," she whispered in his ear, and felt his breath shudder in, his body a humble mix of power and need.

"Not yet."

He grabbed her hand and tugged her down the corridor, shoved open a door and flicked on a light.

The bathroom. An expensive, elegant display of tiling, golden fixtures and a huge spa bath. But it was toward the massive double-headed shower he went, taking her with him. He shoved the glass door open then turned back.

Slowly, silently, he undid her coat buttons, his gaze never leaving hers as he peeled the edges away. After she shrugged out of the coat, he grabbed the bottom of her sweater, dragging it up over her head.

Then his breath came out in an almighty rush.

Thank goodness she had on halfway decent underwear instead of her ratty old sports bra.

The chain-store brand white satin push-up created the illusion of cleavage, shoving her breasts up into a seductive silhouette and, judging by Chase's expression, was worth every penny.

His hands went to her waist, fingers splayed over her skin and Vanessa shivered.

His eyes snapped up to hers. "You're beautiful."

She felt the heat rise in her neck and she swallowed, smiling shyly. "Thank you."

"Dunbar was a grade-A jerk."

She shrugged. "I know." She slipped her arms around his neck and leaned in, silencing him. "But do you really want to talk about him? Or would you rather..." She brought her mouth to his ear and whispered, "Take my clothes off and get wet?"

When she took his earlobe between her lips and nibbled, a deep groan was her reward.

Oh, yes. His arms snaked around her, pulled her flush against him and she gasped. Yes.

He was rock hard and she was eager to get naked. He obliged by sweeping his hands up and over the swell of her breasts, palms running over the mounds before gently digging around in the cup and popping one free.

She gasped aloud as he wasted no time on niceties, simply took her nipple into his mouth and sucked.

His mouth was hot, wet and so very good. His tongue did crazy things to her skin, whirling around that hard nub of flesh, tasting and teasing until her knees began to buckle and her breath came out in small pants.

He did the same to her other breast, hand in cup, mouth on nipple, while he massaged the other, his rough hands creating a flurry of sensation that rose with every passing moment.

Their ragged breaths echoed off the walls, interspersed with Vanessa's gasps when his teeth rasped over her sensitive nipple. Her entire body felt wired, as if Chase had somehow set her very blood aflame. His arms tightened around her, bringing her closer to him, to the hardness that pressed insistently into her belly. It made her insides flutter, crazy with anticipation.

He was still taken with her breasts, his tongue running over first one puckering nipple, then the other, tweaking them gently with his fingers then his teeth, his muffled appreciation hot against her sensitive flesh. She shuddered, shifted from one foot to the other as the heat between her legs became uncomfortably warm.

"Chase," she whispered, then hitched in a breath as his hand swept over the small of her back to settle on her jeans-clad bottom. She felt his mouth curve, pressed up against one swollen breast.

"Mmm?"

"Please." She finally looked down…and sucked in a gasp as she met his eyes over the swell of her breast. His lips parted and his tongue flicked out, licking her nipple as his gaze boldly held hers.

"Please what? Please do this?" He bared his teeth, grazing her responsive flesh then grinning as she shuddered. "Or maybe this?" His lips pursed and he blew gently on the tight nub, sending another tremor racing down her back. "Or…this?"

He shifted one knee, swiftly thrusting it between her legs, and Vanessa gasped at the intense pleasure coursing through every intimate part. His hand followed, cupping her through the denim, and he shuddered.

"You're warm. So incredibly warm." With skillful fingers he plucked open her button fly, his lips on her neck. She held her breath, her head spinning as his fingers grazed her through her panties.

"Take these off."

He'd read her mind. She quickly kicked off her boots then wriggled out of her jeans, shoving the entire mess across the tiles before she eagerly returned to him.

He dragged her in for another kiss, the heat searing her nipples into painful nubs. She tried to ease herself by rubbing across his chest, but it only made things worse.

She felt him chuckle, his mouth on her neck.

"I fail to find my discomfort funny," she breathed.

"Discomforted, are you?"

He nibbled her collarbone and she shuddered. "Very much."

"Then I'll have to fix that."

His hand went to her panties, his large palm cupping her warmth, drawing out a sigh from her.

"Open your legs, Vanessa."

It was a shockingly intimate command, but one she immediately responded to. His fingers drew the elastic aside and dived down, parting her curls, then her most intimate folds.

She sucked in a breath then let it go in tiny stutters. Inch by agonizing inch, with his gaze locked on hers, he gently slid inside her.

Everything trembled, her heart spilling over into almost painful ecstasy. "Chase, please!"

In response he captured her mouth with his, stifling her protest as he gently rocked her forward then back, his fingers deep inside her as the palm of his hand rubbed and teased her engorged flesh.

And that's all it took, a divine moment, Chase's hands and mouth and suddenly she was there, right on the edge, and the view was breathtaking, everything she'd expected and more. Yet before she could find sweet release, he withdrew.

Her eyes sprang open, a protest on her lips, but in the next instant he reached inside the shower and turned on the faucet full blast.

His eyes, dark with passion, locked onto hers as he quickly stripped, the water pounding down behind him. How had she ever thought he was closed off, devoid of emotion? It was practically sizzling from him, barely contained beneath all that smooth muscle and a multitude of internal scars.

And when he was finally naked, she let out a slow, steadying breath.

He was all hers.

"Come to me," he said softly.

She did.

Chase nearly lost it right there. Her red hair spilled over her shoulders, that ridiculously sexy bra bunched down to her waist, revealing the most beautiful set of breasts he'd ever seen. They fit perfectly in his hands, those dark pink nipples just right for his mouth. She tasted amazing, of passion, lust and innocence rolled into one.

As the steam began to spill out from the shower and swirl around them, he leaned in, placed a kiss on one nub and grinned as he heard her breath jag in. Her nipple puckered and tightened under his tongue, and he groaned. The air grew heavy with the scent of desire and he looked up to see the flush creep up her cheeks again, her lips still plump from his kisses.

"I'm all yours, Vanessa. Now, let's get wet."

He went slow, even though his body was desperate for completion. He undid her bra and it fell away, then with both hands he tugged her into the shower. Water crashed down over him, then her. As it soaked her hair, ran over her shoulders and breasts, he placed soft kisses along every faint line the bra had made on her skin, his fingers following the damp trail as Vanessa sighed in pleasure.

He slowly nibbled her hip bone, loving the way she moved beneath him, her murmurs of encouragement, eager for more.

He hooked his fingers in the waistband of her soaked panties and slowly, sensuously, slid her wet underwear down her thighs, past her knees until he finally tossed them to the tiles.

He skimmed her calves, ran his hands back up her legs then her thighs. A gentle mass of red curls lay at the juncture and he breathed in her womanly scent, cupped her bottom then looked up.

She was looking straight down at him, water cascading over her face and shoulders, rivulets coursing around her breasts, one thin stream peaking over the tip of her hardened nipple. He was so aroused he burned.

Until she shifted, parting her legs, and Chase stopped breathing.

They both paused in that moment—an eternity—and their eyes clashed, widened.

"Chase… My coat. In the left pocket…" She bit her lip, looking so adorably uncomfortable, so imperfect, that his heart cracked open a little bit more.

"You always carry condoms in your coat pocket?"

Her blush stretched his grin wider.

"No. Just for you."

When her eyes, her oh-so-serious eyes met his, he nearly crumbled.

Stepping outside the shower, he grabbed her coat, rummaged in the pocket with wet, trembling hands. Finally he pulled out a foil packet, ripped it open and attempted to pull on the condom, cursing softly as anticipation made him clumsy.

Her hand on his shoulder stilled him. "Let me."

He turned, the sting of frustration battling with embarrassment, but she simply smiled, took the condom from him and expertly eased it over his throbbing length.

His breath seared his lungs and he fought for control. Damn.

He couldn't wait any longer. With a groan, he nudged her against the shower wall, wrapped one of her legs around his waist and pushed deep inside her.

Vanessa flung her head back with a triumphant cry and every muscle, every vein in her body dissolved in pleasure. She tightened her arms around him, her heavy exhale-inhale on his neck giving him trembling pause before he slid halfway out, then plunged back into her warmth with a wrenching groan.

His blood sang. He filled her totally, completely and his senses reeled from overload—slick water on their skin, the murmurs of pleasure and his name on her tongue, bathing him in sweet desire. And the incredible, amazing...*excruciating* joy of making love to her.

He was exposed and raw, every inch of skin sensitive and throbbing for her touch, so he crashed his lips on hers with a satisfied groan then thrust his tongue into her mouth. She writhed against the tiles and met him, mimicking his movements, possessing *him*, claiming *him* in the most primitive way possible, sending his blood rocketing. He shifted his weight, hands beneath her bottom as he yanked her other leg around his waist. When she locked her ankles at the small of his back, he rocked into her, keeping time, pushing deeper, faster, until ecstasy began to well inside.

Chase tried to hold back, but through the haze of passion, he felt her muscles clench him and knew she was nearing climax. Even though his legs were screaming and his arms ached, he gritted his teeth, gripped her bottom and kept going.

Almost there… His breath huffed out, the water battering his shoulders and back as deep inside, the familiar swell of release began to gather and tighten.

"Chase…" Her eyes sprang open and those wide green depths, riddled with ecstasy, unmanned him. They stared deep into his very soul, bearing witness to the most intimate of embraces as he spilled himself into her with a wrenching groan.

His hands went to the wet tiles, desperately trying to hold them both up as he shuddered over and over.

Good Lord, that was…incredible. He buried his face into the crook of her neck, tendrils of her fiery hair clinging to his cheek. She throbbed and pulsed around him, her skin slick against his, her nipples digging into his chest. When she tightened her embrace with a soft sigh, he closed his eyes and stayed right where he was, determinedly ignoring the cramp that had set up in his legs.

Eventually, regretfully, he withdrew. In silence they soaped each other up, rinsing off under the steady stream before Chase finally turned off the faucets.

They dried each other, at first tentatively, then with slower, knowing strokes. Those strokes became touches, then kisses, then Chase was pulling her into the bedroom. Vanessa caught a glimpse of luxurious carpet and heavy brocade drapes in the dimly lit room before they got to the crumpled bed.

Then he commanded her entire focus.

He sat on the bed and pulled her close to stand between his knees, then began at her ankles.

As his large, firm hands smoothed over her calves, massaging the muscle beneath, her breath hitched in pleasure.

"Feel good?" he murmured, his voice husky.

"Oh, yes."

"Just wait, it gets better."

She matched his grin with one of her own. "Oh, I'm sure it will."

He dragged his hands up to her thighs but wasted little time there, preferring instead to cup her bottom, kneading and squeezing as his breath got heavier and more ragged.

It stunned her, this kind of power she had over a man like Chase. He could have any woman he wanted and yet he wanted her, was aroused by her, Vanessa Partridge, working single mother of two.

Thick desire surged, making her impatient and eager for his touch. As if sensing her mood, Chase's hands stilled and his gaze went to hers, eyes dark with passion.

"I want you."

That just about undid her, her entire body taut as she did as he asked.

"Come forward. Put your knees on the bed."

She was way too wired, her skin aching for him, the anticipation building to an unbearable level. How she managed to get her legs on the edge of the bed, she'd never know. But she did and soon Chase had eased them around his waist while his manhood throbbed hard between them. Then he shoved his hands under her bottom, lifted her up, maneuvered her until she was poised above him and their breaths mingled for excruciating seconds while they kissed.

He took his time kissing her: long, deep, lingering kisses with lots of tongue and hot breath until every single cell in their bodies pulsed with urgent desire.

Without warning he plunged her down and her sharp cry of ecstasy bounced off the bedroom walls. He filled her completely—so hard, so hot. Every inch of skin where they connected was wet with desire, from their eager mouths, to their torsos, to deep inside her very core. When he gripped her, rocking her back and forth, back and forth, a groan of pleasure ripped from her lips, quickly silenced as he covered her mouth with his.

Yes. Oh, yes. She moved with him, her arms wrapped around his neck, hips rocking, lips devouring, the air punctuated with sensuous sounds of skin on skin and murmurs of desire. And soon, she began to feel the glorious waves of orgasm swell.

Then Chase stopped.

Her eyes sprang open on a groan of frustration. "No! No, keep going!"

Chase clenched his teeth as she wriggled against him. "Wait. Stop, baby. I need to—"

To her shock he pulled out, then quickly flipped her on the bed.

Vanessa dragged herself up on her elbows. "What are you—"

"Shh." He put his hands on her knees, stilling her. "You'll like it, I promise."

"I liked it the other...ooooooh!"

He'd pushed her legs apart and his mouth had fastened onto the most intimate part of her sex.

Everything exploded, her hips bucking off the bed in shocked delight. His tongue licked long, languorous stokes, whipping her up into a frenzy of desire. And just when she thought she could take no more, his teeth grazed across those swollen folds and she cried out in rapturous joy. With her head flung back, her fists clenching the sheets and Chase's tongue diving in and out of her wet core, she came.

She barely had time to recover, the shudders racking her body before she felt him slide up, his lips on her belly, over her waist, before pausing to lick one peaked nipple.

Bliss. He massaged her breast, his warm palms rubbing each hard nub into almost unbearable hardness. And heaven help her, she was still aroused by that. And when he spread her legs wide and slid inside, a deep sigh of contentment rushed out.

He filled her up physically, mentally, spiritually. It was almost a divine experience, having him move inside her, watching the play of emotion across his face as she stared deep into his eyes. His breath bathed her skin, his mouth swooping down for a lingering kiss.

They made love slowly this time, like two familiar halves of one whole. Each caress, each kiss, anticipated, welcomed and returned. And when Chase eventually achieved release, Vanessa reveled in the comforting intimacy of his body pressing hers into the bed, his throbbing manhood still buried inside her.

It felt like an eternity had passed before Chase finally slid from her. But instead of moving away, they remained in a tangle of limbs, staring up at the ceiling in groggy exhaustion.

Gradually, the gentle sounds of their heavy breathing slowed and the air began to cool.

She could lie like this forever, with nothing but his damp skin and their intimate scent perfuming the air.

"Come with me to New York," he said suddenly.

She blinked and met his serious eyes. "What?"

He pulled back on his elbows. "Come with me to New York."

"This weekend?"

"No, right now."

She laughed. "Are you being funny?"

Chase remained silent and unsmiling.

Oh. "You're serious." Her head began to spin. "I need to get up." Her hands went to his chest and slowly, agonizingly, he pulled away from her.

Her body cried out at the loss and she dragged her knees to her chest, wrapping her arms around her legs. "Chase, I can't. I have a job. And the girls."

He reached out and brushed a lock of hair behind her ear, making her shiver. "Bring them with you."

She shook her head. "No."

He stilled. "Why not?"

"They're babies and need routine with minimum disruption. I can't spring a new city and new people on them without prep-

aration. And I've already left them twice in a month and…"
She sighed. "I can't drop everything and run off with you."

He frowned. "I'm not asking you to drop everything."

"So what *are* you asking?"

He dragged a hand through his hair. "I'm asking you to come with me to New York. Does it have to be more complicated than that?"

Ah, but what if she wanted complicated? What if she wanted something more than just a fancy New York trip? What if she wanted Chase permanently in her life?

But that's not what he'd offered.

Vanessa's stomach twisted in uncomfortable realization.

"Chase, I can't just up and leave my job on a whim. I won't."

"A whim." His expression clouded. "I see." When he pulled back, her heart pounded in worried alarm. "I shouldn't have jumped to conclusions and assumed you'd want to spend some time with me."

Her heart pounded in alarm. "I do! But there are other things to consider too, like my job, and how it will impact on the girls."

His eyes narrowed. "You don't want me in their lives?"

A wave of anger hit her and she swung her legs to the floor, dragging the sheet to her in swift jerky movements. "That is not what I said! But you're assuming a lot when I can't afford to—"

"I have money, in case you've forgotten."

"And that's *your* money, Chase. Not mine. And anyway, this isn't about money. You're expecting me to drop my commitments and I spent too many years living under my father's roof to—"

His face darkened. "I am not your father."

"Then stop acting like him!"

As soon as the childish, hateful words were out, she wished she could stuff them back. But the damage was done.

They stared at each other in shocked silence, until Vanessa stepped forward, clutching the sheet to her trembling body.

"Chase—"

"No, I get it." He reached for a pair of pants and jerked them on with cold, painful dignity, snapping the fly together swiftly. "It's fine, Vanessa." His sharp bark of contemptuous laughter made her flinch. "I guess I should've seen it coming. Someone like you—" his eyes scathingly raked her from head to toe "—and someone like me. It'd never work."

"Chase, please! You're—"

"You need to leave." He shot her one last look then strode over to the bathroom, slamming the door behind him.

And Vanessa was left confused and alone, the room growing ever colder as her heart silently shattered at her feet.

Twelve

Chase woke slowly, reaching out to where Vanessa should have been and finding only an empty, cold mattress. His eyes sprung open and he sat up, glancing over at the clock—9:10 a.m.—then dragged a hand through his hair as last night came crashing back.

She was gone.

His heart plummeted, the solid beat echoing the tight throb in his head.

Damn. With a groan he swung his feet to the carpet, took a deep breath and stood.

His world remained a jumbled mess, even as his breath began to return to normal and memories flooded in. The feel of skin. The dark passion in her eyes. Her beneath him, surrounding him, filling him.

Already half-aroused, he fell back on the bed with a curse.

And that stupid, pointless argument.

He was in love with Vanessa Partridge. The signs were all there: he'd trusted her with Sam, with his past. Yet he had no clue how she felt about him, and that awful, gnawing uncertainty came with a whole bagful of awkward emotions.

It was as if he was a kid all over again, fearful of expressing himself, afraid of mediocrity, terrified of rejection.

So he'd gone and rejected her first. What the hell did it matter where he lived as long as Vanessa was with him? As long as they were happy?

But now she'd probably never speak to him again.

He lay there for a few more minutes, sifting through everything, reliving those awful words, until his head began to throb in earnest.

Do something.

He tightened his jaw. He was a man of action, not a boy of doubt. An apology wouldn't cut it—he needed a big gesture. And he knew exactly what he had to do.

He rushed through a shave then a shower, the memories of last night still fresh on the warm tiles. Charged with purpose, he dressed then called down to the lobby.

"I'll bring the contents of your safe up to you personally, Mr. Harrington," the day manager replied, "along with your breakfast. I trust your stay with us has been satisfactory?"

"Very much."

"That's excellent. Is there anything else I can do for you today, sir?"

"No, thank you."

After Chase hung up he made a few phone calls and was checking in with his office when the knock came.

Anticipation surged as he opened the door, revealing a waiter and the neatly suited day manager. As the waiter laid his breakfast tray carefully on the table, the manager—Ryan Kwan, his badge indicated—stood to one side, hands behind his back.

Chase hung up. "You have my package?"

Kwan swallowed, his shoulders as rigid as a soldier at attention. "It appears, sir, that the contents of your safe are... ah...missing."

Chase stared at the man for one uncomprehending second before a swell of fury quickly overtook it.

"What the hell do you mean—*missing?*"

Kwan swiftly dismissed the hovering waiter then closed the door behind him. "If I could verify your safe number?"

Chase reeled off the number, barely able to keep a tight rein on his growing anger.

Kwan nodded then said, "If you would follow me downstairs, Mr. Harrington…?"

The seemingly endless elevator journey only chewed away the last of Chase's thin control. A bunch of innocent scenarios had already been reviewed then rejected—mistaken safe number, accidental removal by staff—but instinctively he knew this was definitely not an accident.

So who on earth knew he was here and knew he had the manuscript with him? Who wanted it so badly?

Vanessa did.

Everything ground to a halt the moment that terrible thought popped into his head. But still he considered it, examining the facts from every angle, dissecting the scenarios then put it all back together.

No.

He finally discarded the thought outright, but the damage was already done.

Even if they hadn't spent last night heating up his bed, he knew her. She'd been with him, by Sam's side, for nearly two days, and he'd gotten to see a side of her that he somehow knew had always been there, if he hadn't been so blinded by her former life and all his prejudices.

So why the hell had he even suspected her, even for a second?

The elevator doors slid open and as he followed the manager across the foyer, a dark cloud of realization began to build, poisoning his thoughts.

Because you can't trust anyone. Because your life is a to-

tally screwed affair, thanks in part to the hand you'd been dealt as a kid.

He'd spent years running away from that kid, drowning out the memories with money, power, success.

If he could think that of Vanessa, there was something seriously wrong with him. He sure as hell didn't deserve her. She'd be better off with a guy who'd trust her implicitly, someone who wasn't always suspicious of everyone and everything around them. Who looked at people with open honesty instead of waiting for them to betray, humiliate or leave him.

Who are you to deserve someone like Vanessa?

"Ness, you've checked your messages three times already! Can you just put that thing down and enjoy having lunch with us?"

Vanessa placed her phone on the table with a sigh, glancing from her sister to an amused Ann Richardson while the lunchtime bustle of her favorite local café swirled around them. "That's rich coming from you, Jules."

"Yeah, but all mine are work-related. I hardly think you're about to get called in on an emergency diaper-changing."

Vanessa pointedly ignored her sister's lame joke and turned to Ann. "So, you're going to Rayas. Gorgeous country. Near Dubai, right?"

"Yes," Ann said. "But there's no time for sightseeing—it's a business trip."

"Anything to do with those golden statues?" asked Juliet. "I read about them in the paper," she added at Ann's look. "One's missing, along with your treasure hunter, right?"

"Roark's official title is acquisitions officer, but yes, that's right."

"I met him once, a few months back at that party of yours, remember? Totally gorgeous, but," she added to Vanessa, "a bit too dangerous for my liking."

"Oh, Roark is a perfectly decent guy," Ann countered.

"So why doesn't he have a girlfriend?" Juliet asked.

When Ann shrugged, Vanessa offered, "Maybe he's just too busy. Or he hasn't met the right girl yet."

"He's a scoundrel," Juliet said with a sniff. "I like perfectly decent men."

"Ha!" Ann laughed. "Sometimes you need a scoundrel in your life. Especially a gorgeous one."

"Yeah, I think you've had enough of those, sweetie," Juliet said dryly. "And speaking of gorgeous... I hear your Rayan sheikh is rumored to be a bit of a hot one. Raif something-or-other."

"Sheikh Raif Khouri. Crown prince of Rayas. And I suppose he is attractive if you're into the whole 'dark and mysterious' thing." Ann began spooning her pumpkin soup with way too much intent.

"He's single?"

"Yes."

"Sooo..." Juliet placed her chin thoughtfully on her steepled hands. "Any chance of a little romance while you're there?"

Ann gave her a look. "No."

Vanessa weighed in, glad Juliet's single-minded attention had focused elsewhere. "Gorgeous man, romantic country..."

"And is he a scoundrel?" Juliet grinned.

As they all laughed, Vanessa made a surreptitious glance at her phone again.

"...and there's Australia. A long flight, of course, but lots of men to—oh, Ness, will you just call the guy and stop fiddling with that phone?"

Vanessa snapped up to meet her sister's narrow look.

"So out with it." Juliet sighed. "He's the one you flew to Georgia to see, right? Who is he?"

"No one you know."

"You sure? I know a lot of people."

"Trust me. You don't." She couldn't help but flick a glance at Ann, who was listening to their to-and-fro with an amused smile.

"What does he do?"

"He runs a hedge fund."

Juliet's eyebrows went up. "Well, well. You've got yourself a rich man. I take it he *is* rich?"

"Yes."

"And? What's his name?"

Vanessa's gaze went first to Ann, then back to Juliet. "You are *not* going to check up on him."

Juliet held up a hand. "I swear to God, that's Dad's shtick. Not mine. Now, out with it."

Vanessa sighed. "His name is Chase Harrington. He—"

"The guy who won the Dunbar auction?" Ann interjected.

"Yes."

"Hmm."

Ann left that hanging, until Juliet took up the slack. "What else does he do?"

"He works, he spends his money, he donates to charity."

Her sister frowned. "Is that all? What about other interests outside work? What do you two talk about?"

"Lots of things." Vanessa felt the blush rise at the memory of one particular intimate conversation.

"And," Juliet added with a direct point of her fork, "what do you have in common?"

She stumbled her way through a few answers, yet when Juliet went back to her salad niçoise, Vanessa mulled over the questions again.

She knew Chase lived to make money and was committed to the Make-A-Wish Foundation. She also knew what truly motivated him, which made him different from all those other men who didn't care about the deeper consequences of amassing a fortune. He had a conscience. An inner drive. He was a man whose experiences and deep-held beliefs had shaped him into the success he was today.

And she also knew he made love like a god fallen to earth.

Hunger now gone, she toyed with the remaining pasta on her plate.

Was she that forgettable? Was his grief and anger so huge

that it completely overshadowed last night? She'd thought it had been an amazing, breathtaking night, but obviously…obviously…

Chase hadn't thought so. Because he'd been swayed by one stupid argument.

She'd called him twice and had gotten his voice mail twice. The third time, she'd hung up before it had clicked through again. Dammit. How could they work things out when he refused to even talk to her?

She sat there, glaring at her phone even as her heart began to crack.

Well, it was his loss if, after one argument, he decided he didn't want her.

The jerk.

That thought burned a hole in her stomach, until the ache of it all began to make her feel sick.

"I have to get back to work," she said when the waiter appeared with the dessert menu. She gave him a small smile and stood. "I'll take a latte to go." She turned back to Juliet and Ann. "You both stay. Continue catching up, okay?"

"Okay," Juliet said. "But you know we'll be talking about you as soon as you leave."

Vanessa grinned, her mood lightening. "You always do." She leaned in and kissed her sister's cheek, then Ann's. "Have a safe trip. I hope it's a successful one."

"I'm sure it will be."

Despite Ann's confidence, Vanessa could still detect a faint sheen of worry behind her eyes, which was odd, considering Ann was such a strong personality and totally in control of everything she did and said.

Although not lately, judging by the papers.

"Let me know how it goes," she said impulsively, her hand still on Ann's shoulder. "Okay?"

Ann patted her hand, smiling. "Sure. I'll call you."

With her take-out cup firmly in one hand, Vanessa made

her way back to work, sad in the knowledge that Ann probably would call her. Unlike Chase.

On Thursday, Chase had had enough of staring blankly out at the breathtaking New York skyline sunset from his apartment window. Instead, he threw on his running gear, headed down to the second-floor gym and for sixty solid minutes, ran on the treadmill until he'd left every churning thought in the dust.

For the past four days the familiar sting of failure had tainted everything he did, creating a bitter aftertaste that only infuriated him more. He'd thrown himself into the usual flurry of phone calls, texts and emails, keeping a close watch on the stock market, his regular websites and TV stations. Yet his orderly brain demanded answers, answers that were frustratingly lacking.

He hated failure and this one was worse than any tanked business deal—this was personal. A thousand times worse. He'd not only failed Mitch and Sam, but now he could add Vanessa and her girls to the list.

He grabbed a towel and wiped his dripping brow. The papers had exploded with the missing manuscript story hours after the police had been called to the hotel, so he'd had the fallout of that to deal with too. After two grueling days of dodging the press, he'd finally managed to return to New York, to the relative peace and quiet of his apartment.

Past the pounding of his heartbeat and his heavy breath, he clicked on the decline button and the treadmill began to level out with a smooth whir.

Vanessa had called his cell phone three times, but every time, left no message.

Which meant she'd changed her mind about talking to him. *He* wouldn't want to talk to him, either, not after the way he'd left everything.

You're afraid of seeing her again, aren't you? Afraid of facing her disappointment, knowing he was the one who'd lost that manuscript. And knowing he couldn't do a damn thing about retrieving it.

Every day meant another rumor, another speculative guess as to who the thief was. The one currently doing the rounds was that Ann Richardson was behind it all.

Waverly's CEO, a criminal mastermind? Damn ridiculous. From what he'd been hearing of the woman—credible sources, not the tabloids—there was absolutely no reason for her to jeopardize Waverly's reputation or her own by committing a felony. In fact, she had way more to lose.

And Vanessa trusted her, which meant more than second-hand reports.

As his stride slowed and the treadmill began to power down, he swallowed the rest of his water then grabbed his phone.

A handful of missed calls, work stuff...and a familiar number. Anticipation surged as he redialed the ex–Rushford colleague who now worked on the *New York Times* front desk.

"Mal, it's Chase. What have you got for me?"

"Well, for one, the rumor that Ann Richardson was behind the theft? False."

"Yeah, I was kind of thinking that."

"And the good news is they found out who stole your manuscript. Does the name Miranda Bridges ring a bell?" Mal said.

"No. Who's she?"

"Dunbar's publicist. She's been dating a guy whose brother is currently in Rikers for homicide. The feds have linked *him* to a bunch of ex-cons, including a thief and a fence. And the trail from them led back to a night-desk guy working at the Benson the night before your manuscript was discovered stolen. The whole lot were arrested a couple of hours ago."

"They were professionals."

"Looks like it. The feds are already linking them to a bunch of other high-profile thefts in the Washington area."

Chase ran a hand over his eyes. "And the bad news?"

"You know me too well. Your manuscript has already surfaced on the black market. The lead in your case is trying to track it, but it'll take some time. And even then, these people use aliases to bid. The chances of recovery are slim."

"So it may be gone after all."

"It was insured, right?"

Chase sighed. "Yeah. But that's not the point."

"Sorry I couldn't have better news."

He remained standing on the now-silent treadmill long after he'd hung up.

He'd done what he'd set out to do, which was to fulfill Sam's wish, and despite what he'd told Vanessa, that achievement did bring him enormous satisfaction. Yet somewhere along the line he'd decided he had to fulfill Vanessa's wish too. Failure—an old, familiar feeling—cut as deeply now as it had years before, when he'd been fresh from the Rushford Investment fiasco.

And just like before he needed to focus on the things he could control. Which meant work. Making money.

He jumped off the treadmill and headed for the shower with grim purpose.

An hour later, Chase walked into his corner office, the lights still on. The view from the window was identical to his apartment's, one floor above: a breathtaking nighttime panorama of the city with the Empire State Building center stage and red taillights streaming down Madison Avenue. He'd gotten into the habit of turning off all his apartment lights and drinking in the perfect photographic scene, marveling at just how he'd gotten here.

Tonight, however, it wasn't the view that commanded his attention.

A thick envelope sat on the corner of his desk. He grabbed it, turning it over.

It was addressed to him, no return address.

With a smooth flick of his finger, he opened the flap, reached inside then stilled when he pulled out the familiar sheaf of papers.

Dunbar's manuscript.

His heart sped up, thumping hard against his ribs and he

tossed the package on his desk, strode to the door and yanked it open. He swept his gaze down the short corridor, first left toward the elevator then right, to the darkened office on the other side. Nothing was amiss and no one was about. His assistant had long gone for the day, the cleaners yet to arrive.

"Hello?" he said into the cavernous silence, then paused, listening.

Nothing.

He went back to his desk and read the attached note:

Chase: This came up on the black market. You earned this back. Now give it to its rightful owner—little owners, I should say.

It wasn't signed.

He dropped his hand and the note fluttered to the floor. Who on earth would do something like this? He knew lots of people who could afford it, but none he'd peg as a charitable donor, especially now with the notoriety attached to the manuscript. They were all too selfish for that.

Vanessa was the only person who came to mind, yet why would she buy it, then return it to him?

With a frustrated sigh, he collapsed into his chair.

He had no idea who was behind this or why they'd spent a bundle getting back the manuscript. But he did know what he was going to do next.

Thirteen

Vanessa stood in the school kitchenette, trying to soothe a crying baby while a feeding bottle warmed. When Stella strode in, heading for the fridge, her back pocket suddenly blared the familiar strains of "Route 66."

"Hey, Stell, could you do me a favor and get my phone? It's my sister."

As Vanessa grabbed the bottle from the warmer and tested it on her skin, Stella reached into her pocket and pulled out the cell phone.

"Shall I tell her to call back?"

"No, I've been waiting for her call. Can you take Darcy?"

Once Stella had left the room with the squalling infant, Vanessa wiped her hands on her jeans and swiftly swiped open her phone.

"Jules. Where are you?"

"Back in L.A. Has Ann rung you?"

Vanessa walked out into the play area. "No. What's happened?"

"The FBI is searching her office, that's what! They reckon

she's hiding information about the missing statue. And with Roark missing and unable to corroborate her story, it's all over the news."

"What channel?" Vanessa strode into Stella's office, clicked on the keyboard and pretty soon she had CNN streaming live on the screen. "Got it."

In silence they both watched the news snippet in its entirety.

"Unbelievable," Juliet finally breathed down the phone. "I got Dad to give me a few names, but apparently Waverly's already has some hotshot lawyer on retainer."

"Well, with all their problems, I'm not surprised." Vanessa reached for the mouse and was about to click away, when the next news item caught her eye.

She froze on the spot as her heart dropped to her toes.

"Ness? You still there?"

She swallowed thickly. "Are you seeing this?"

"What, the arrest of some guy for the theft of D. B. Dunbar's manuscript?"

"Yeah." Again they both lapsed into silence and watched.

"Wow," Vanessa breathed when it had finished. "What a mess. So Dunbar's publicist was behind it?"

"I think she was just as stunned, judging from her reaction when the press ambushed her."

"Did you know the manuscript had been stolen?" Juliet asked.

"Yes, I saw it on the news when the story broke."

"So Chase didn't tell you?"

"No," she said softly, picking up a pen and putting it back into the holder.

"Hmm."

"We're kind of not speaking at the moment."

"Hmm," Juliet repeated ominously.

Vanessa frowned. "I know that tone."

"And what tone is that?"

"That 'tell Juliet all about it' lawyer one."

"Uh-huh."

"There's nothing *to* tell. He… We…" She sighed as the

lump in her chest made its way up to her throat. "It was just a thing. Not serious."

"He gets you to fly down to Georgia for the weekend to meet the people in his life, you spend a night with him and it's not serious? Babe, that's as serious as a heart attack."

Vanessa choked back a sudden chuckle. "Serious as...? Where do you get this stuff from?"

"Been watching a lot of Samuel L. Jackson," Juliet replied, then Vanessa heard her shuffle a few papers. "That man is so fine. Like your Chase but, you know, a wild and crazy fantasy."

"Yeah, well, at this point, mine kinda is, too."

Juliet sighed. "You always have *the* worst luck with men, Ness. First those weird grungy guys in college, then James the jerk, then Dunbar—"

Vanessa stilled. "What?"

"D. B. Dunbar. You know, the father of your children?"

Vanessa swallowed, an automatic denial on her lips. Then, with a sigh she said, "How did you find out?"

"Oh, I had my suspicions, but didn't know exactly *who,*" Juliet said breezily. "I only figured it out after our lunch with Ann. You really should work on your poker face more."

"But..."

"Don't worry, your secret's safe, sis. I'm discretion with a capital D." She paused then added gently, "You've never talked about Erin and Heather's father, and I never pushed you to, either. You always did play your cards close. But if you ever feel the urge to talk—or need any help—I'm here. Okay?"

Vanessa dragged a hand over her eyes and swallowed the lump welling in her throat. "How did I get such an awesome sister like you?"

Juliet chuckled. "You must have pleased someone in a previous life. Oh-oh, gotta go. I'll let you know how Ann's doing when I know more. Love you."

When Vanessa hung up, she walked slowly from the office and over to a bunch of toys scattered on the play mat. Jasmine and Megan, Vanessa's coworkers, had allowed the children out in the yard, but at the first sign of rain they'd be in. As a consequence, the huge room was empty except for the shrapnel of toys, puzzles and various works of art. She smiled at Lola, their work experience girl, who was currently watching a handful of babies in a fenced-off area, Heather and Erin included.

Three surprises in one day must be some kind of record. Yet despite Ann's problems and Juliet's revelation, they both took a backseat to the loss of Dunbar's manuscript.

Ahh, that cut. A lot. But as she glanced over at Erin and Heather happily playing away with Lola, her lips curved.

Life was good. She refused to be unhappy, not when other people—like Ann—had bigger problems, and many more—Sam, Dylan—had their lives taken away far too early. She'd get over the theft of the manuscript, even if imagining some faceless rich thief pawing at those pages made her ill.

But that brought her back to the loss of Chase.

The overwhelming ache in her heart caught her breath. Such a small corner, the place where she'd shoved all her disappointment and hurt, but she knew from experience it would all fade in time. Eventually.

But did it really have to hurt so damn much?

She determinedly pushed the box of toys back into its spot in the bookcase.

"Um, Vanessa?" Stella said slowly behind her.

"Yes?"

"You'd better look out the window."

Vanessa sighed and straightened. "Don't tell me it's snowing?"

"Not exactly."

Vanessa frowned at Stella, who had a baby over her shoulder and was grinning like an idiot in the direction of their gated yard. "Are the kids going crazy? Do Jasmine and Megan need a hand?"

"Just get over here, woman."

She sighed, making her way to the huge sliding glass doors to peer out. "So what—"

Her words froze in her throat, along with her heartbeat.

A tall, familiar figure stood in the yard, hands in his pockets, next to a row of jittery toddlers, each holding up a piece of cardboard with one letter. All together the sign read:

I ♥ u, Vanessa.

Oh. Her throat constricted as she choked down a sob.

Stella swept the door open and gave Vanessa a gentle shove.

He stood there in complete silence, the kids' excited chatter flowing around them, dark storm clouds amassing against a pure blue sky, making this a scary, surreal moment.

"You called me," he said.

"I know."

"Three times."

"Yes. You were busy."

"You didn't leave a message."

"No."

His mouth tightened into a remorseful line. "I was going to call you on Monday morning but—"

"The manuscript was stolen." She crossed her arms, suppressing a shiver.

"Yes. And I…" He sighed. "I was angry and frustrated and a little ashamed."

Her breath caught. "Of us?"

"God, no." His shook his head. "I was ashamed of losing the manuscript, the one thing that meant so much to you—to your girls. It felt like a huge failure."

"But it was stolen—not your fault."

"Still felt like it."

She uncrossed her arms and shoved her hands into her back pockets with a sigh. She'd practiced this moment over and over in her head, in case the opportunity to take him to task ever arose. She'd be haughty and cold, giving him her best death stare, and reducing him to a groveling, apologetic mess after jumping to that wild conclusion.

It had been a crazy fantasy, one she conceded would probably never happen. And of course, she'd conveniently ignored her part in their argument, when she'd compared Chase to her father. And now, as the week's events came crashing back, all that pain coupled with the pinnacle of ecstasy, her righteous anger fizzled out.

How could she hurt him? Not when he stood before her now, so hesitant and uncertain and surrounded by a sea of chattering, giggly kids, while her colleagues stared in morbid fascination.

With a thick swallow, she finally found her voice. "I thought…I thought you didn't want me."

Chase's stomach dropped as he bit back a soft curse. He stared at her, at every feature, every line and hair. The gentle curve of her cheek, the dark eyelashes that framed wide green eyes, her long neck that was so sensitive beneath his lips. How could he have ever thought she was shallow or superficial? He'd had such a good thing and he'd nearly let it slip though his fingers by allowing his past to choke him of a possible future.

"I can't believe I've been such an idiot," he muttered.

"And I can't believe I accused you of being like my father. You're nothing alike." She glanced over at his kid-and-card sign, her eyes lingering, face softening before she came back to him. "But if you don't kiss me now, I will never forgive you."

Chase's heart plunged sickeningly for a nanosecond then when she gave him a gentle smile, it began to thump hard and fast.

He moved swiftly and with purpose, his eyes fixed on her as he demolished the space separating them. Then his hands were on her arms, her soft sweater and warm skin beneath heating his frozen fingers, her wide smile sending a flicker of desire into his belly.

With a soft groan he leaned down and finally kissed her.

Her sweet breath, familiar scent, yielding lips all swept him up on a tide of emotion, and he pressed closer, desperate to feel her body against his.

He vaguely heard clapping and cheering, and then Vanessa

gently broke away, a blush staining her cheeks as she gave a small self-conscious laugh and glanced shyly at their enthusiastic audience.

Despite her embarrassment, a smile curved her lips.

"Vanessa, you…you see me," he whispered fiercely, gently placing his forehead on hers. "Everything." His eyes locked onto hers, blue on green. "I can't remember the last time I've shared so much with someone. Apart from Mitch, no one knows my real story. It's—" he dragged in a breath "—scary."

"I know." She placed her palms on his chest and everything leapt.

"Remember when you told me we weren't that different?" he said.

"Yes."

"You were right."

He let the silence envelope them, the seconds ticking away until he added, "I don't like to talk about the past."

He could feel the loaded weight of her scrutiny yet she said nothing.

"There were six of them, three jocks and their girlfriends." His mouth curled in remembrance. "I still remember their names even after all these years. They teased and tormented me every single day in high school. I was not a particularly attractive guy, nor was I articulate. My strength was my brain. A brain I used to great effect when I got my first job out of college. With Rushford Investments."

He drew a hand over his eyes as the bitter memories tumbled before he finally let them go. "I worked under a guy called Mason Keating. He was brilliant and I absorbed all his advice as gospel, followed his investments, emulated his practices. He was like a god to me."

"But something happened."

"He ripped off his investors, tried to lie his way out of it then ended up skipping the country. Of course, the company quickly covered it up and struck deals with the investors to keep them from talking. It was never in the papers."

And Chase had walked away, disillusioned and deeply wounded from the experience.

"Every time I feel myself dwelling on the past, I thank God for it. Because if it weren't for that awful broken road, I'd never have met you. Kids?" He turned and nodded at the ones still left, and they obediently turned over their cards:

aMrry me

Vanessa stilled, closing her eyes to savor the moment, the unbelievable burst of hope that began to spread slowly through her veins. When she opened them again, Chase's frowning countenance, threaded with an unfamiliar wariness, forced her breath back into her lungs.

"Say something," he muttered.

"You spelled 'marry' wrong."

With a frown he spun to his little accomplices, but they'd had enough and chose that moment to break ranks, rushing around in the misty rain with peals of delight.

"Brats," he muttered not unkindly.

She made a halfhearted attempt to hide her grin with her hand, but quickly gave up. "Yeah, kids are unpredictable like that."

His gaze darkened. "I missed you."

She inhaled a deep, chilly breath, swallowing as her eyes welled up again.

"I missed you, too. Even though I called you a bunch of bad names in my head."

"Yeah, I probably deserved it for overreacting."

"You did. And I called myself a few, too."

"And I think you deserve this." From the bag at his feet he pulled out a package. Her heart stilled for one second then began to soar in surprised disbelief.

Dunbar's manuscript.

"Oh, Chase. This is… It's…" She stood there like a complete fool, staring blankly at him while her emotions ran riot. "I thought it was stolen!"

"It was. But then it turned up on my desk last night."

She frowned. "How?"

"No idea. Apparently I have an anonymous donor who urged me to return the manuscript to 'the rightful owners.' You know anything about that?"

She shook her head. "No. I don't know anyone with that kind of money or connections. My father might, but he'd never knowingly purchase stolen goods." She paused then said slowly, "I'm sure Ann would know a few people who…ah…skirt the fine line of the law but none who know me. And no one's ever connected me to Dunbar, let alone the girls… Well, except my sister, but she would've told me if she'd done something like this."

Chase sighed, shoving his hands in his pockets. "Okay, so—"

"Hang on. That means someone out there knows about the girls." She gripped his arm. "What if they're planning on doing something else? Like blackmail?"

"Do you honestly think they'd give me Dunbar's manuscript to return, then turn around and blackmail you? When you don't even have any money?"

"That's not the point. What if they go to the press? Or camp out at the school?"

"Then we'll get security," he said. "Or cut them off by drafting a press release. We can also move to France or Sydney where I have a couple of properties." His mouth curved. "I even have a private Caribbean island if you prefer."

"I don't want to run away."

"We're not. We'll just be taking sensible precautions until the attention moves on to someone else."

"But what if—"

"What if nothing happens? What if you're worrying for nothing?" His face twisted. "Vanessa, sweetheart, you're killing me here. Do you want to keep stressing about what-ifs or do you want to give me your answer to my question?"

"What—" Oh. His strained expression, a mix of doubt and dreaded anticipation, did her in. But there was one last thing she had to know.

"We don't have to get married, you know. Because I know how you feel about it, and how it can complicate things…"

"Vanessa." He took her cold hands in his, warming them up. "I want us to be a family. You, me, the girls." His mouth curved into a sexy grin. "Maybe a few more later. And that's a commitment—no, a *promise*. It means I want it—us—to work. And if here is where you want to be—" he swept out a hand to encompass the building "—I promise I'll make it work."

"You'd commute?"

He shrugged. "I do most business via the internet or phone anyway. I'm hardly in my office."

Vanessa shook her head. "But you'd be giving up—"

"Not much. I'd be gaining so much more." Vanessa followed his gaze to the glass doors, to where Lola was standing with Heather in her arms, and watched his expression soften.

Her heart gave a joyful jolt. "It's not going to change you? Us?"

"Not unless we want it to." As she paused, he added with a smile, "I swear, I will let you know if you start acting all crazy on me."

"Like buying expensive manuscripts then giving them away?"

His eyes creased. "I'm not giving it away if it's staying in the family, right?"

She felt the grin crack her face as a breathtaking wave of happiness filled every corner of her soul.

"Then yes, Chase. I will 'amrry' you."

His unfettered look of joy, the blinding smile combined with those amazing eyes, sent her heart soaring. He was finally hers. Every intense, complicated, gorgeous, passionate inch of him. So she kissed him again, just because she could.

"Ah, Vanessa?" Chase murmured against her mouth. "I'm not complaining, but you *do* know we have witnesses?"

"Oh." When she broke off, his chuckle against her lips sent a tremble of happiness from head to toe.

"Hey, you two!"

"Hey, Stella," Chase called back, his gaze still locked on Vanessa.

"Hey, yourself. You ever gonna come in out of the cold?"

He stared deep into her eyes, that fiercely intelligent blue gaze seeing everything, uncovering every doubt and fear until love swelled up, filling every corner of her heart. "I already have."

"You're crazy, you know that?" Stella grumbled.

"Yeah," Chase murmured. When Vanessa suppressed a shiver, he opened his coat, pulled her against his chest and wrapped her inside with him.

The play of soft wool tempered the hard, warm planes of muscle underneath and she breathed him in, unable to get enough of the moment. "But where are we going to live?"

"Wherever we want. That's the beauty of having lots of money—we can make it up as we go along."

Her chuckle dissolved into a sigh of pleasure. "I love you, Chase."

"And I love you, my perfect Vanessa."

That evening, after Stella had offered to take the girls with a knowing grin, Chase stood nervously in the shadowy darkness of Vanessa's bedroom as she drew the curtains, enveloping them in moonlit shadows.

After baring his soul today, he was actually nervous. But those nerves quickly scattered when Vanessa turned and her entire face lit up with a beautiful smile.

"Vanessa," he groaned.

"I love you, Chase. I've loved you ever since Georgia."

Oh, Lord, she undid him every time! She weaved her fingers through his and squeezed gently before placing a kiss on his knuckles. When he searched for her eyes in the shadows, her lips found him instead.

The kiss was soft, tender. Full of emotion and compassion. Just like Vanessa.

When he thought he couldn't be surprised by anything anymore, he felt a great shift inside as his heart opened up to new hope, new possibilities, and the swell of joy that followed swamped every muscle in his body.

"You're so beautiful." He gently peeled her T-shirt up then tossed it over his shoulder. So very beautiful.

He swept a palm over her breast, smiling when he heard her breath catch as her nipple peaked beneath her bra.

"Chase?"

"Yeah?" His mouth swooped down to tongue that hard nub, grinning in satisfaction as a shudder coursed through her.

"Talk to me…" She hesitated, her eyes flitting to him shyly, then away. "In that accent of yours."

He swallowed, dragging the soft cotton of her bra cup down past the swelling peak. "You like it?"

"I do."

He grinned. "Sure thing, ma'am."

Another ripple of pleasure shimmied down Vanessa's spine as he gently pushed her back to the bed.

"I can feel your nipples pushing against my mouth. They're so hard, like tiny pebbles. And I ache so much…" He glanced up, eyes capturing hers. "Can you feel me?"

She swallowed. "Yes."

Their gazes met, held. When Chase reached for her hand and gently placed it over her breast, she groaned aloud.

"Tell me what it feels like," he murmured.

"It's hard…" She swept her palm over the bud, sucking in a breath when her body involuntarily jerked. "Yet so soft."

His mouth went to the underside of her breast, gently lipping the sensitive skin. "Tell me what you're feeling, Vanessa." His voice had gotten deeper and that sexy drawl, nonexistent on a normal day, had now stretched his vowels into a perfectly arousing tool of seduction. "Tell me everything you're doing."

She swallowed again, her throat dry, and sat heavily on the bed. "Can you…keep talking?"

His deep chuckle had her squeezing her thighs around his waist, trying to stop the flood of sensation escaping too soon.

"Sure thing, darlin'." He paused then said, "Lay back and run your hand over your skin."

"Yes." She closed her eyes and let his voice and her hands take her away.

"Cup the fullness. It's warm, isn't it?"

"Mmm."

"I can taste you." His heavy sigh washed over her, tightening her insides. "I'm going to take one of those plump nipples in my mouth and suck it until you're writhing beneath me."

Oh…my. The bed dipped beside her, then his hot mouth suddenly fastened onto her peaking nipple and she would've jerked clean off the bed if Chase's thigh wasn't pinning her down. He simply chuckled and kept right on teasing her, using his tongue, mouth and hands until she was indeed writhing beneath him.

He straddled her, then paused. As the warm silence flowed around them, Vanessa wasn't sure if it was her heavy breath she could hear or his.

She watched him swallow thickly, his eyes black with passion. "Can you feel that?"

"Yes." *Inside me, outside me. Everywhere.* She reached between their slick bodies and grasped the full hard length of him. When he groaned and gave a shudder, she just about combusted right then and there.

He was all hers. Right now and forever.

"Are you wet for me?"

She knew the answer without even going there, the throbbing heat proof enough. "Yes."

"Open for me."

It took just three little words, three deep, sexy words drawled into her ear to make her lose all her inhibitions. As her mind spun and her breath held, she spread her legs and Chase smoothly thrust inside her.

He stilled and a sigh escaped, a soft, contented sound that came from deep within his soul. Her insides tightened and soared when she wrapped her arms around his neck, pulled him down and kissed him. His heart pulsed against her bare skin, matching hers as their tongues danced and he murmured warmly against her lips. Everything throbbed, from her skin to her mouth, to the more intimate core inside. He filled her completely and she was hot and aching for him.

And then slowly, slowly, he began to move and she dissolved into flames of pleasure.

Chase's hypnotic voice coaxed and encouraged as he told her in exquisite detail what he was going to do to her, with her. And she was completely wrapped up in every word, every shockingly sexy description, every hot breath. He had her so tightly wound that it barely took a half a second for her release moments later.

Her back arched as the orgasmic waves washed over her. She was unashamed, not caring that her cries of ecstasy reverberated through the still room. Moments later, she felt Chase stiffen then join her in the final throes of passion.

Minutes passed, the air punctuated by their ragged breaths as they gradually returned to earth, and Vanessa slowly opened her eyes.

"Wow."

He chuckled and shifted, his arms tightening around her. "Wow yourself."

"It was…"

"Perfect," he finished.

His warm breath on her forehead finally slowed and his lips trailed softly across her cheek, the intimate tenderness gripping her heart and twisting it.

She breathed him in, absorbing every damp inch of his passion-laden skin, every intimate throb as he remained inside her.

"I love you, Chase."

"And I love you, Vanessa. Always."

And right there, right now, everything really was perfect.

* * * * *

*Turn the page
for a special bonus story
by* USA TODAY *bestselling author
Barbara Dunlop.*

*Then look for the next installment
of* THE HIGHEST BIDDER,
*THE ROGUE'S FORTUNE,
by Cat Schield
wherever Harlequin Books are sold.*

THE GOLD HEART, PART 4
Barbara Dunlop

Six months ago

Aimee Khouri might not have a royal title, but her father, Sheik Ghani Khouri, was twenty-sixth in line to the throne of Rayas, so her wedding was taking place in the grand hall of Valhan Palace. Preparations had been under way for months. The guest list was over a thousand. And it had taken her seven hours today to bathe, dress and do her hair and makeup.

Aimee wasn't as attractive as her two sisters, Cala and Zahra, and she couldn't hold a candle to her third cousin, Princess Kalila, who was second in line to the throne. But Aimee felt beautiful today. She wore the traditional seven-layer bridal outfit of colorful silks and satins, sexy lace and gorgeous ribbons. She couldn't wait for her groom, in keeping with Rayasian tradition, to slowly peel them away from her body tonight.

Handsome and urbane, her groom, Daud, belonged to a family who owned Rayas's largest shipping company. He'd been educated in Britain, so he was more progressive than most Rayasian men. No autocrat husband for Aimee, no traditional rules or expectations. She'd spend her life visiting the great ports of the world, wear western clothes, attend glittering social functions and meet interesting people.

Alone for a few final moments, she paused at the end of the central palace hall. At exactly four o'clock, the massive double doors to the great-hall foyer swung open, revealing the rest of the bridal party, her two sisters, four other attendants and her father. Happiness settled deep inside Aimee's chest.

Her father nodded to her in silence. No one would speak now until the chancellor started the ceremony. The attendants took up their positions in a diamond formation around her. Their ice-blue gowns set off her own top robe of deep purple satin and the royal gold-and-white scarf that flowed around her head. The purple robe was parted at the front to reveal the mauve lace of her full-length dress. Beneath that was a shorter dress, with cap sleeves, and on it went until the gossamer camisole that would be Daud's final reward before they made love tonight in a private tower of the palace.

She moved forward, swallowing delightful butterflies of excitement. But, halfway across the foyer, her gaze was distracted.

The large, glass dome that sat on a marble table in the center of the rotunda was empty. She blinked, wondering for a split second if it was a joke. But she quickly realized nobody would remove the Gold Heart statue as a prank, particularly on a royal wedding day.

"Father?" she whispered.

"Shh," he commanded.

"The Gold Heart," she warned him. "It's missing."

"Shh," he repeated, his tone stern.

"But—"

"We will discuss it later."

Aimee's stomach cramped. "Where did it go?"

Had somebody moved it? Was it in the great hall? A new tradition perhaps?

Her sister Cala moved close behind. "It was stolen," she told Aimee quietly.

Aimee's gaze flew to her father, encountering his stony profile. "No," she rasped, horrified.

"Hush," he ordered.

She stopped still. The Gold Heart statue was the family's talisman of love. It had been that way for three hundred years. Three statues had been carved to protect the three daughters of the ancient king. One had been lost a hundred years ago, and the romances in that branch of the family had been doomed ever since.

"They are looking for it," her father assured her.

"How can I get married?" she asked in a strained whisper. This wasn't right. This wasn't fair. She was minutes from a marriage to a perfect man.

"Do not worry," said her father.

"But—"

"They will find it."

"In time?"

He smiled, a rare event. "What is in time? You are young. Before your honeymoon is over, the statue will be back."

Aimee's stomach relaxed a little. Her father was right. The king would move heaven and earth to recover the precious statue. Everything was going to be fine.

She began walking again, passing through the royal archway and into the grand hall where well-wishers from around the gulf and beyond had gathered. She saw Daud in the center of the room, on a dais beneath a glittering gazebo. He looked nervous, even more nervous than she felt. He also must have heard of the statue's theft.

He wore traditional white robes. His scarf was emerald green. Next to him, his boyhood friend and prime attendant, Jacx, was resplendent in the black dress uniform of the Rayasian navy.

Jacx didn't look remotely nervous. His features were fixed, the slash of a mouth, the square chin, his sculpted brow were hard as ice. By contrast, his dark eyes looked molten with anger. Aimee could guess why. He resented participating in the wedding. She and Jacx had never liked each other. He found her opinionated and frivolous, while she found his relentless traditionalism extremely tiresome.

Unlike most of the Rayasian upper crust, Jacx hadn't traveled abroad for university. Instead, he'd attended Rayas's military academy. Sure, he'd graduated at the top of his class, and at twenty-seven he had already achieved the rank of captain commanding a royal ship. But he was set in his ways, fixed in his thinking, and likely couldn't have laughed if his life depended on it.

Her wedding party reached Daud. Aimee's leading attendants separated to let her through, and her father stopped, letting her go forward on her own. The string music faded, and she moved to her groom.

Daud's brow was damp, his hands clasped together. His gaze had darted to her, taking in her dress, her scarf, her ceremonial gold jewelry. She waited for him to meet her eyes.

"Your Royal Highnesses," the chancellor began, bowing to the king and to the princes and princesses in the front row. "Honored guests," he continued.

Daud shifted his feet.

"This is a glorious occasion." The Chancellor paused for a dramatic moment. "For thousands of years, people have come together at Tibalta—"

Daud said something under his breath.

The chancellor gave him a sharp look. "On the full moon of spring."

Daud whispered something that sounded like "I can't."

This time, the chancellor glared an unmistakable rebuke. "In the presence of our king."

Aimee tried once again to catch Daud's gaze, but he was staring off into space.

"I can't," he repeated. This time, there was no mistaking his words.

"Can't what?" she found herself asking.

Finally, he looked at her. "I can't marry you."

"Because of the statue?" she asked.

He blinked in what seemed like confusion. "What statue?"

It took a moment for the meaning of his words to sink in. When they did, a roaring started in Aimee's ears, and her fingers began to tremble. It wasn't the Gold Heart? It was something else? Daud was calling off the wedding?

It was a nightmare. It had to be a nightmare. Oh, wake up. Oh, please wake up.

Daud turned to the king, bowing in deference. "Your Majesty. To my deep regret, and utter sorrow, I must confess, I love another."

A collective gasp went up from those in hearing distance.

Aimee's legs turned to jelly. She would have collapsed, except a strong arm slipped around the small of her back. She didn't look to see who was there.

The elderly king rose, and all the room's occupants stood with him.

"Explain yourself," he boomed, his voice stronger than Aimee had heard in many years.

"I love another," said Daud, dropping his head.

"You are pledged to Aimee."

"I know," Daud admitted.

"You would put emotion before duty?" the king demanded. Daud nodded.

The king's jaw went tight, anger darkening his eyes.

"Wake up, wake up, wake up," Aimee ordered herself under her breath.

Crown Prince Raif Khouri whispered something in the king's ear.

The king frowned at his son. But his next words were for Daud. "Her family will require compensation."

"Of course," Daud answered, his relief embarrassingly obvious. He bobbed another bow. Without a single look to Aimee, he backed from the dais.

A gray haze moved in front of Aimee's eyes. A blessing, since it saved her from seeing anyone in the crowd, her parents, her sisters, heads of state, news reporters who would recount the salacious details for days and weeks to come. The murmur started low, at the back of the room, but then it rolled forward as people whispered to their neighbors.

And then a voice rose above the din. "Your Majesty, the wedding can continue."

The king stilled, and Prince Raif's gaze fixed on Aimee. No, not on Aimee, on a spot just above her head. She glanced up to see Jacx. His jaw fixed, sheer determination in his dark eyes.

"The wedding can continue," he repeated, his fingers tightening where he grasped her waist.

The breath left Aimee's body.

"You will do your duty?" Prince Raif asked.

"I will," Jacx intoned.

"No," Aimee coughed out. It might be tradition for the prime attendant to step in, but it hadn't happened in over a hundred years, certainly not at a royal wedding, and definitely not at hers. She wouldn't be bound to Jacx, a military man, a traditional man, a man who would leave her marooned in Rayas while he went off to patrol the seas for his country.

"Shut up," Jacx muttered.

"I will not," she insisted.

"The wedding shall continue," the king decreed.

"You can't—"

Before she could get another word out, Jacx deftly spun her around to face the chancellor. His hand moved to clasp firmly over her mouth. He put his mouth next to her ear. "Do not contradict your king."

Aimee tried to speak. She tried to push away. She understood that Jacx had just saved the honor of her family, of the royal family, of the king himself. But she couldn't marry Jacx. They hated each other. Rayasian marriages were forever. There was no such thing as divorce. And, most important, he didn't know the terrible thing she'd done.

Everyone seemed to make a collective decision to ignore Daud's outrageous behavior. Outwardly, it came off like any other wedding. People danced and laughed and congratulated the couple. The king made a ceremonial presentation of an antique sapphire necklace, a heritage piece from the royal collection, as a wedding gift. Jacx smiled stoically, if falsely, through the entire charade. Aimee was numb. She didn't remember reciting her vows. Maybe she hadn't. Maybe everyone was simply going to pretend she'd spoken.

People's voices made no sense. She couldn't decipher the words. The music was a cacophony in her ears, and she only danced mechanically when Jacx dragged her onto the floor. She made the mistake of looking into his eyes. Something burned there, a possession, an anticipation that she feared she recognized. With Daud, she had been safe. With Jacx, she was in insurmountable trouble.

He was going to see her naked. He was going to do what every other groom did on his wedding night. He would discover her deepest, darkest secret. And he would use it against her. She knew very well he would use it to destroy her.

Her stomach was a knot of misery as they rode away in the traditional, horse-drawn carriage, to the cheers of the guests and the good wishes of the king. At the east palace tower, it was a short climb to the third floor, a modern suite with a sofa grouping, a big dining table, a massive en suite bath and a huge, four-poster bed strewn with rose petals. The windows were open, and the ocean breeze buffeted the gauzy curtains. The lights were low, vanilla-scented candles burning on the tables next to the bed.

As Jacx shut and locked the door, Aimee took a step backward, then another, and another.

When she forced herself to speak, her voice shook. "What have you done? Jacx, why?"

"Duty," he answered simply, no expression on his face, no inflection in his tone.

"Duty?" she rasped. "You're stuck with me."

And she with him. She had to get out of this, get away from him somehow.

She glanced to the open window. If she threw herself out, it would all be over. Problem solved. Troubles behind her.

She could hear the waves crashing on the rocks below. Would it hurt? Would death be instantaneous?

"What would you have had me do?" he asked.

"Nothing," she all but wailed, knowing she wasn't going to be able to kill herself. That meant she'd have to confess to Jacx. Maybe he'd kill her, take the decision out of her hands. Nobody would blame him.

"The king would have been embarrassed in front of his guests, royalty and businessmen from the entire region."

"You did this for the king?"

He moved closer still. "I did this for my country."

"Will you get a promotion?" She struggled for some logic in his decision. "A medal?"

"Likely." He came to a halt less than an arm's length away. "The king will never forget, and Prince Raif will never forget. Marrying you is my ticket to success."

It was dark humor. They both knew the statement was ridiculous. Jacx was a legendary soldier and sailor. He was already in command of one of the military's most important vessels. He'd risen far in the ranks for his age, and there seemed no end to his military career.

"There is one other thing." He reached out to touch the shoulder of her purple gown.

He moved so fast, she didn't have time to flinch.

"I get you," he said, fingering the thick satin.

Her mouth went dry.

"Seven layers?" he asked, a meaningful glint in his eyes.

Aimee's heart rate redoubled.

He slipped the open gown easily off her shoulders. It slithered to the floor, revealing the mauve dress beneath. Then he pulled back her scarf, releasing her long, dark hair, tossing the scarf in a blur of white and gold onto the nearest armchair. She fought a bubble of hysterical laughter. Even in these bizarre circumstances, Jacx did not let the royal colors touch the floor.

The front of the mauve dress was fastened with ties, delicate, white ribbons, for the groom to savor as he pulled them apart, one by one. It should have been Daud, not Jacx. She felt tears burn her eyes.

"Don't bother," Jacx told her harshly as the mauve gown fell to the floor.

Next came ivory satin. Beneath that was fine silk, each layer thinner and more revealing than the last.

She sniffed.

"Crocodile tears will gain you nothing."

"I'm not—" she started to protest.

She wouldn't try to manipulate him with tears. She didn't think there was a single thing she could say or do that would sway such a harsh man. She was his wife, and he would treat her like the property he considered her to be.

The ivory satin dress was short, only to her knees, revealing her calves, the satin wedding slippers, and the ribbons that crisscrossed their way up her thighs. The dress was also sleeveless, ties at the shoulders, to be undone so it dropped away.

Jacx stared into her eyes, one hand untying each delicate bow, easily, swiftly. The little dress fell away. There was nothing but thin silk between them now. Her knees were bare, and he glanced down at the length of her legs.

"Jacx, please," she begged. Though she wasn't sure what she wanted. If not tonight, it would be tomorrow, or the day after. It did her little good to buy time in increments of hours.

He didn't seem to hear her. The backs of his fingers ran the length of the silk, along the side of her breast, her rib cage, her narrow waist, the curve of her hip. His touch left a trail of warmth, sensitizing her skin, increasing her pulse, tightening her chest to a band of uncertainty. She needed him to stop, wanted him to stop, wished he would stop. Didn't she?

"Beautiful," he breathed.

It wasn't clear if he meant the fabric or her. And she wasn't going to ask. If she asked, it would mean she cared. And she didn't care if Jacx thought her beautiful. She didn't care at all. The tip of her tongue found her bottom lip, and she bit down against the unaccustomed heat.

He flicked the garment over her head, tossing it.

When he reached for her again, she grasped his hand. His nostrils flared, lips flattening. "You would fight me?"

"I…" She stumbled, tears forming once more. "I…"

He cupped his palm around her shoulder. His tone was guttural. "I did not do this to get another promotion. Not to win another medal. I do not want the king's or the crown prince's favor."

She swallowed, trying desperately to find her voice, to force herself to blurt out the words that would seal her fate. "Jacx," she managed to say.

His eyes flared with desire.

"I am…" She closed her eyes. But that was even more frightening than watching his expression. She opened them again. "I am not…" She clenched her fists, gathering her strength and her courage. "I am not a virgin."

A full minute passed in excruciating silence.

His hand dropped from her shoulder, and she flinched, trembling, steeling herself for his action. At best, he'd throw her out, humiliating her family, turning her into a pariah. At worst, he'd kill her, a defiled bride, one not worthy of keeping.

"Daud?" he demanded, tone flat.

She gave a shaky nod.

"When?"

She didn't understand the question.

"When?" Jacx barked.

"Two weeks ago," she blurted out. "The wedding was so close. We were practically married. There was no reason…" Her voice trailed away.

"That son of a bitch," Jacx spat.

Two tears of terror escaped from her eyes, rolling down her cheeks. "Will you kill me?" she sobbed.

He popped the buttons on his uniform tunic, stripped it from his body and tossed it aside. In his shirtsleeves, he confronted her.

"No," he said.

"You will throw me out." She accepted his decision with resignation. In some ways, she thought death would be easier.

Jacx moved closer, voice going lower. "No," he said.

She blinked, not understanding.

"I will have you." He reached out to tug off the next layer of silk and lace. "You are mine, and I will have you."

She was thoroughly confused. "And then discard me?" She told herself it didn't matter. What did it matter? Her virginity was gone. She was ruined anyway.

Jacx grasped her upper arms. "I will keep you."

"As your mistress?" There was a fate worse than death.

"As my wife."

"But I am not fit."

He tilted his head to one side, his expression and tone going unexpectedly soft. "And who will know that, Aimee? Who will there ever be to say?"

"You will know." She searched his expression. Was he toying with her? Was this a cruel joke?

"I'll tell no one. You'll tell no one. And Daud will tell no one. I guarantee that."

She was utterly confused. Jacx wasn't going to ruin her or kill her? He was going to protect her secret, accept a bride who had lain with another man? How could Jacx, of all people, display such compassion?

Unexpectedly, he drew her into his arms. He held her there.

"Would it help to know," he whispered into her hair, smoothing it back, "that when Daud backed out on you, it was the happiest moment of my life?" His voice went hollow. "I grabbed onto you in that second, and no force on earth was going to take you away. If he'd recanted, begged the king, I would not have let you go."

Aimee struggled to decipher Jacx's words. They weren't making sense, but there was a sense of security in his arms that she didn't want to give up. She wrapped her arms around him, clinging tight, imagining for a moment that everything was going to be all right.

"Prince Raif saw it," Jacx continued. "He knew enough to give you to me."

Aimee tipped her head back, gazing at Jacx's rugged, handsome face, looking, really looking at him for the first time in her life. "But you don't like me."

"I don't like you with Daud."

"I make you angry."

"Because you were with Daud. Every time he whispered to you, touched you, made you smile, I wanted to rip him apart."

Comprehension shaped Aimee's lips in a silent oh. "I have misjudged you?"

"I made you misjudge me. I'm not what you think, Aimee. I am not a monster. Will you trust me? To make you happy?"

A lump formed in Aimee's throat. "It's you who cannot trust me. I slept with Daud," she felt honor bound to remind him.

"It does not matter."

"How can it not matter?"

"He deceived you. He coerced you." Jacx smoothed her hair again. "You will forget him. I am going to make love to you so long and so hard and so thoroughly that you won't even remember his name. We're leaving Rayas. We leave tomorrow on a three-month voyage."

Aimee took her first full breath in hours. "I can come on your ship?"

"I am not leaving you here." He leaned in and pressed his lips to hers. They were soft, supple, the pressure perfect, her body's reaction electric. Arousal she'd never felt before zinged from the roots of her hair to the tips of her toes. She parted her lips, and the delicious sensation increased. Her arms wound around Jacx's neck, her silk-covered body molding naturally against his.

His palm slipped to her bottom, pressing her against him. He was steel and strength, determination and honor. And he'd been there for her when her life was about to end.

She drew back, gazing up at him, open, honest and grateful. "I will learn to love you, Jacx," she vowed.

"I will love you," he returned. "And I will show you the world."